CODE NAME: AZRIEL

To the rebel underground she was known as *Juanita,* field commander of the United States Army of Rebellion, a brilliant leader skilled in the arts of guerrilla warfare.

To Bo Bevis, Lieutenant Commander of the rebel stronghold in South Florida, she was an enigma—a beautiful, driven woman with a shattered past, who fought the Enemy and shared his bed with equal passion.

But she was also known as *Azriel,* the Angel of Death—a cold, ruthless spy and saboteur who executed traitors with her own bare hands.

Whatever she was, she was the key to the rebellion. Without her, it would not succeed. With her, it could not fail.

THE AZRIEL UPRISING
by Allyn Thompson

Bantam Science Fiction and Fantasy Books
Ask your bookseller for the books you have missed

THE AZRIEL UPRISING

BY ALLYN THOMPSON

BANTAM BOOKS
TORONTO · NEW YORK · LONDON · SYDNEY

THE AZRIEL UPRISING

A Bantam Book / April 1982

ISBN 0-553-20487-4

Published simultaneously in the United States and Canada

Bantam Books are published by Bantam Books, Inc. Its trademark, consisting of the words "Bantam Books" and the por-
trayal of a rooster, is Registered in U.S. Patent and Trademark
Office and in other countries. Marca Registrada. Bantam
Books, Inc., 666 Fifth Avenue, New York, New York 10103.

I

The bright yellow GM school bus lurched cheerfully from side to side on the rolling road, urged on by merry passengers. What a fine day for some sightseeing! Sun shone warmly on these California hills year-round, to be sure, but even here the sun knew springtime was the best time, and its light had an added amiability.

On the side of the bus—below the windows eager faces were pressed to, cameras held against—black letters used to read "Marin County School System." Now that was covered over with Cyrillic lettering, so most of the people who saw the bus from the roadside couldn't read it. But the new, cruder stenciling said "Army Recreation Department."

The passengers were very, very glad to have a little time off.

Occupation duty was hard. You were shipped thousands and thousands of miles away from home to a place you'd been told was the essence of evil and danger. The occupied territory was vast. Oh, the commanding officers told you it was nowhere near as big as the home country—but if you were from Moscow, had you ever been to Tashkent? Did a boy from Kiev have to move to Kransnoyarsk for two years?

So the Occupied Territory seemed huge and threatening indeed, even if thousands and thousands of kilometers of it were declared off limits.

And the *people* of the Occupied Territory, well, they were worse than a mystery to the men and women of the Red Army. They had a terrible violent streak that emerged just when you had them most expertly supervised. They would go along acting properly, doing as they were told, even responding to rather strong orders. And then, something small, like the command's call for identification tattooing and—poof!—they exploded into riots that required strong measures to put down.

What's more, these people weren't even all alike. They were white, black, red, yellow...and all dangerous.

The sides of the road were lined with waving wildflowers, and every once in a while from a hilltop, there was a view of the ocean, looking left. Oohs and ahs greeted the sea, and cameras clicked faster.

The bus slowed a bit as it passed a sign in English, a small black-on-white sign on a tall post. "What does it say?" the passengers asked each other.

The bus driver knew the route by now, and said, "Bodego Bay. We are entering the town called Bodego Bay."

From the stand of birch trees and scrub evergreens, you could see Route 1 for a long way south, excluding the dips in the road. "Juanita" sat Indian-style on the ground, not moving a muscle, her mind equally still. All details of the plan were as well arranged as they could be, and she had learned there was no profit in worrying. If you could stay calm, affairs were apt to go your way, because the opposition usually panicked.

She checked herself from the top down...neck relaxed, back flexible, calf muscles smooth. She wiggled her bare feet, looking at the thick, cracked calluses on the soles for signs of irritation, or cuts.

There was a little sound, like a bee's buzz, and she cocked up her head to look through the greenery. Silence for a moment, then the buzz built up again, and the yellow bus snouted up over a hill and careened down into the next valley. "Juanita" tapped a couple of sticks together, three times, and a small dark boy popped up from the gulch on the other side of the road. Looking behind him, he put his finger to his lips.

But the suburban neighborhood was already still. Even the dogs that usually skulked around the rusted-out Buick or, smelling food, pushed their muzzles against old screen doors, made no sound.

The buzz of the bus became a full diesel-engine roar. It hove into view over the last hill before Bodego Bay, and pulled into what the dilapidated English sign referred to as a scenic view. There was a groan of brakes, a hydraulic gasp, and the bus door opened.

The occupants spilled out, laughing and shutter-clicking in their green-brown uniforms. They inhaled the fresh ocean air, enjoyed the view, and took yet more pictures of themselves— "With Yuri, my friend"—"With Stolev, whom I wrote you about"—in Occupied Territory.

The small, dark boy ran across the roadway to the pull-off, his hands outstretched in a plea, his language Spanish-accented.

"Comrades, comrades, have you anything for me and my friends?" And a small horde of children skipped from behind the hill.

The men and women of the Army just loved children, and they began to ransack their pockets, bags, briefcases for treats to give the little ones. An especially angelic blonde girl even coaxed the bus driver from his seat, since she was too shy to come inside for a chocolate.

"Juanita" slid out of the bushes, across the road, and under the bus, holding something that looked like an unbaked loaf of bread in her right hand. The asphalt was crumbling, and almost as noisy as the gravel of the pulloff. Diving head first under the engine, she was slapping the plastique to the exhaust pipe before she stopped skidding. The explosive clung to the corroded metal but, for insurance, she taped it on with two strips of electrician's tape from her left forearm. Blonde hair left the skin with the tape.

She was digging her heels into the gravel to get back out when she heard the driver's heavy feet climb the steps overhead. She slid over on her stomach, and clawed and scrambled down the spine of the bus, out from the back, and over the low white railing at the sea's cliff edge.

A few passengers drifted toward the bus, their Agfacolor shots of the Pacific sufficient to satisfy even parents land-locked back home in the Caucasus. The oldest tourist, who also was a senior Sergeant, called, "Time we were going," and the rest boarded. The GM engine snorted, chugged in a regular beat, and the bus door closed. It pulled back out onto Route 1, California, Occupied Territory.

300 meters north, the bus exploded in a ghastly stew of metal and flesh and blood. "Juanita" waited for any further noise, then began to shinny up the cliff face. The small, dark boy was grinning at her from a perch on the railing.

"OK?" he chuckled.

"More than OK. Superbo." This "Juanita" had a terrible gringo accent. "But now you must tell everybody to hide very, very deep."

"They will make trouble for us, we know." The boy climbed down fom the railing as "Juanita" swung over it. "What will you do?" The woman was looking at the blast she had made, and the boy could see reflected flames flickering in her pale blue eyes.

"I will hide, too." She turned and smiled, but she still looked very frightening. "I will go somewhere else, and kill more of them."

The boy laughed out loud, ran across the road, and vanished behind a wrecked M-60A2 United States Army tank. Juanita slid back into the brush, and began to work her way south on hardened feet.

2.

If you listened to the official broadcasts of the occupation command, you would have thought the C-zones were cordoned off from the rest of the country by a wall of steel. Reality was much simpler. Some three or four kilometers short of where danger really began—where radiation counters began to signal ominously—signs were posted in a haphazard manner.

There was no exact border. No barbed wire fence. The occupation command had trouble enough getting their troops to post distant-warning signs, much less erect a barrier. C-zones were the modern hellfire and damnation, even for the soldiers of the occupation, who had not seen the cities on fire. Officially, the occupation command ignored the areas. As far as they were concerned, they occupied the entire country, from Maine to Mexico, from sea to shining sea. (Alaska, Hawaii, and Puerto Rico were still a problem.)

Juanita was headed for the Florida C-Zone. Or, more simply, Florida. The whole state was supposed to be hot.

Therefore, it was safe from Russian attack. It had natural food supplies, clement weather—and was close to a major occupation command post.

"If Florida is such a great place, how come the High Command is in New Hampshire?" Juanita wryly asked the Loyalist Commander in Lubbock, Texas.

The Commander didn't want to be flip with a Brigadier General, even if she was a barefoot blonde, but he had an honest streak. "Maybe they don't believe their own propaganda."

"No shit. What other news, besides my orders?"

"There was a border skirmish with the Canadians last week. Sault Sainte Marie."

"And?"

The Commander realized that this Juanita wasted no words. "Canadians chased them off, but the Toronto government made their Moscow ambassador apologize, and court-martialed the C.O." Juanita made an impatient noise and turned to look out the hut's window, across the bleak terrain. Lubbock was the far western edge of the C-zone created by the bombing of Fort Worth, Dallas, San Antonio, and numerous military installations that Texas congressmen had been proud to snare for their districts. Things would have been fine here for the rebels and Loyalists, but there wasn't enough food—too hard to farm without Russian overflights spotting them.

"How are you doing?"

"Us? Well," the Commander shrugged his shoulders, "you can see. It's too much trouble to come in and get us, long as we don't make too much trouble. A little theft of food supplies here, a little gun hijacking from the warehouses there, some slogans on the wall . . . that's about all we can manage."

"How many troops?" Juanita turned, and the Commander realized her blue eyes were almost freakishly pale. Was she some kind of albino?

"Between two and three hundred, depending on how our food supplies are, and whether the Russkies are running a new work draft."

"Guns? Ammo?"

The Commander laughed. "That's one thing's never been a problem in Texas. Every damn warm body who turns up here

5

comes with his or her own arsenal. We've got it all, from rabbit guns to sixty-millimeter mortars."

"You've got a lot of women?"

The Commander shrugged again. "They took away most of the men. I'm sixty-eight."

"Yeah. Well." Juanita turned restlessly back to the window. "I better get it in gear."

"Everybody here would sure be proud to know Juanita came by," the Commander ventured. "You're an underground legend, all of them you've killed..."

"And I'd be a *dead* legend, if everybody knew me and my life story," Juanita said curtly. The Commander finally recognized her speech pattern—the Northeast. Oh, Christ, he thought, and I was about to ask where she came from.

"Well, General, you're not leaving here without some food to help you along." He opened the door, and bellowed. In minutes, a young Chicana brought a wrinkled brown paper bag, wrapped tightly around its contents.

"*Muchas gracias.*" The *rubia* had an atrocious accent.

"*Vaya con Dios,*" the Chicana said, because the Commander was obviously wishing this one off on a long and dangerous voyage. Ay! every voyage was dangerous, now.

The long plains twilight was beginning, making the wiry trees and dusty ground look almost soft and charitable. Juanita slid soundlessly from the cluster of huts and headed east for the river.

The Commander waved goodbye, but she did not look back.

The occupying power was reviving the American railroad system, because even they did not have enough gasoline or jet fuel to move supplies as the extravagant Americans had once done. The roadbeds were rotten, but conscript work crews were fixing them up rapidly. You could ride almost anywhere in a Russian-run train at high speed—without jumps, jolts, or derailments.

And since the occupying power's trains always left behind schedule, they ran at top speed, trying to make up time and avoid work demerits.

Clinging to the gritty undercarriage of a coal car, Juanita

thought grimly about the Depression hoboes she'd seen only in the movies. She hoped the Russians had not seen those pictures: the railroad guards banged on flatcar axles with crowbars, to see if anybody was hitching a free ride to a new job. Which, she reminded herself even more grimly, is what I'm doing.

How would she know where the Russian-delineated C-zone started, and it was safe to move?

When a station sign read "Bay Minette" she knew they had circled Mobile. So it was gone. Or hot. Pensacola, too—probably. Christ, did the High Command have any idea what really existed, and what was obliterated in the war? They'd told her with assurance that the Gulf Coast was almost clean.

The train crossed the Apalachicola far inland, how far she couldn't tell. She guessed it was headed for Tallahassee. From there, if the idiots in New Hampshire knew *anything*, she could walk to the C-zone, and the Loyalist camp.

When the train slowed down to accommodate a rusty Y-switch, Juanita flung herself from the undercarriage onto the gravel roadbed. She could feel skin tearing on her face and forearms. Curling up fetus-style, she rolled down the embankment and, before she reached the gulch, sprang into a running crouch and plunged into the morass of palmetto bushes and water oak. Fifty feet inside, she clambered to the center of a palmetto clump, cutting more skin. Then she froze.

The train was still rumbling over the faulty switch with screeches and groans. Then the caboose clunked by, and rattled into the distance. Now nature started to make its own noises. Birdcalls, slitherings, pops, and hisses. Snakes? Was it far enough south for coral snakes? Scorpions she knew about already, from Texas. The soles of her feet were tough enough, but a scorpion got her on the ankle one night when she was hiding outside the Russian installation on Matagorda Bay. She was hardly able to get going the next day.

Juanita carried no luggage or knapsack, because then they could tell you were on the move. (It had been so long, she never even thought of purses any more.) She wore a man's khaki campaign jacket, with four big expanding pockets, and everything she owned at the time was in them. She pulled a bandanna out of one pocket, a battered tube of Russian petroleum jelly out of another, and began to work on her cuts. Moonlight flickered through the foliage, and her watch said four hours till daylight. Then she would head southeast, guided by her cherished compass.

For some reason, downtown Wacissa, Florida had been burned to the ground. No bombing, here, no craters or impact debris. The trees stood lush and green around the burned-out strip of stores. The parking lot around the ruined Piggly Wiggly supermarket was guarded by a cadre of burned-out cars, and the drive-in movie screen was charred to a stooping skeleton.

And no people. No Russkies. No work farms. No scavengers or outlaws. She must be near—maybe even inside—the C-zone.

All the High Command's orders had said about the regional Loyalist command was that it was last reported on the Suwannee River, between the towns of Ellaville and Dowling. Juanita conjured up a memory-picture of the last map she'd seen, and aimed to hit the Suwanee River—before the war, I would have seen a joke there, she thought humorlessly—directly between the towns.

It would be forty miles from Wacissa, she estimated. She crossed rotting tarmac roads, and circled abandoned houses, always alert for any food or goods she could scavenge. An overturned shopping cart outside a 7-11 store yielded a rusty tin of sourballs. And she found a chisel, plus a box of BBs in a tumbledown garage that still housed a 2-tone Ford Fairlane with tires decomposed to black gum.

The man with the M16 saw her before she saw him, because Juanita was moving, and he was not.

He squatted down for cover, and she heard the rustle. Juanita threw herself flat, and began to slither around behind whoever made the noise. She knew it was no animal.

The man with the M16 raised his head to look again. The whitish hair had vanished. It could be a Russkie deserter, living off the land. He rose cautiously to a medium crouch, and took a step forward.

Something hit him from behind, slamming into the muscles at the base of his neck on either side. His hands opened reflexively, and he dropped the gun. Another blow landed at the base of his skull, but he didn't know that.

When he was aware of anything again, he was face down in sandy soil, eyeing a cluster of fat, frisky Florida ants who were eyeing him back. He tried to roll over, and realized his hands were tethered behind his waist. A foot slammed down on the base of his neck, making it hurt even worse.

"*Tovarich, tovarich,*" he moaned, hopelessly aware that his uniform was regulation United States Air Force. The foot stomped his neck again, and a gun barrel—his own, god-damnit!—prodded his kidneys. "Hey, I'm on top of fire ants here, for Christ's sake." Now he was angry. "You trying to kill me?"

"Identify yourself." Jesus, it was a kid, a young boy! And he spoke good English!

"I'm ... uh ... Beauregard."

"Your name and your unit." The boy jabbed him again.

"Beauregard Bevis, Lieutenant Colonel, United States Air Force," he inhaled and took a chance, "presently attached to the United States Army detachment at Ellaville." The foot and the rifle slipped away, and the Lieutenant Colonel rose with all the dignity he could muster. "Holy shit!" It was a girl!

"Sorry," she said, grinning. "But you scared me. I'm looking for your camp."

"Why?"

"I've got messages from all over. New Hampshire, Texas, Michigan—that's my job. I'm supposed to see Commander Shanahan."

Grumpily, Beauregard Bevis waggled his hands at her. The girl dropped the snout of his M16 toward the ground, and made a turn around sign. As she got near enough to untie his knotted belt, he saw she was older than he'd thought. "Identify *yourself.*"

"Donna Wallace."

Threading his belt through the loops, he saw she was impatient to be moving. "What's your hurry?"

"Running messages, you learn—it's better not to be any place too long."

"Relax, sister." He brushed sand from his tunic. "You're

sixty miles inside the zone. We haven't seen a Russki yet."

"Yeah, well, *I* have. This area hot?"

"This way," he gestured, and the girl/woman pulled out a compass and nodded to herself. "Hey, where'd you get that?" With a crooked grin, she flipped the compass over to show him the inscription. Russian. He started walking.

"I said, is it hot here?"

"You're so well equipped, maybe you've got a Geiger counter to find out," he snarled.

"They would have hit Jacksonville, Gainesville, Lake City..." she recited softly.

"Not Lake City." Bevis dodged some kind of slimy thing he didn't want to think about.

"Ahhh," she nodded in enlightenment. "Which leaves the area pretty cold."

"We're not mutating yet," he snapped. She chuckled. "Hey, mind if I ask, since you mugged me so well..."

"Yeah?"

"One, can I have my gun back? And two, where are you from?" He noticed she never lost her footing, even when she was looking the wrong way. The woman silently handed him his M16, opened her jacket and pulled out a murderous-looking black automatic pistol. Bevis recognized it as a Walther P1. "There's one," she said, plodding ahead. "And the answer to two is—the United States of America."

With no more words, they labored their way through the cypress roots, mud, chokegrass, and Spanish moss.

3.

It took the rest of the daylight to reach the edge of what had been open cattle-grazing land. The crossbreed Florida Brahma Bulls had thrived here by the thousands. But the blasting lights in the sky, the *Gotterdammerung* thunderclaps, and rocking ground stampeded them when the war came. The herds charged the electric fences that didn't work any more, and ran off in the swamps to die. The wiry grass and scrub plants now were waist high.

Bevis saw Donna Wallace sniff the air. "The river?"

"How'd you..."

"Smells like shit." He recalled uncomfortably that the camp *drank* from the river.

"The camp's—there?" Her finger pointed uncannily to the greenery that hid the Number Three guard post. All he could do was nod, and step forward with as much assurance as he could muster.

The code word for his recon tour was "Green Bay Packers." He hoped they wouldn't shoot him because he didn't return alone. There was a whistle that could have been a bird, but wasn't. "Green Bay Packers," he hissed.

"Who you?"

"Bevis." The woman leaned forward and chimed in.

"Messenger from the High Command, for Commander Shanahan."

"Proceed." The guard prudently stepped aside, then followed with his M16 at the ready.

There was about a hundred yards of semi-tropical forest to cut through. Almost impossible for a body of men to cross silently, without clearing the underbrush.

Then they could see lights. Open fires. Kerosene lamps hung from porches, and inside the cabins. Sounds of people—Americans—living, eating, bickering. The woman froze. Bevis tugged on her shirtsleeve. "C'mon."

"Music!" she said, and she was smiling.

"Where you been, lady? Of course—music." He tugged again, and she followed him toward the Commander's cabin, reluctantly leaving the sound of a wind-up Victrola scratchily rendering "Charmaine" by Mantovani and His Orchestra.

The Commander lived in a former sharecropper's hut. It was quite luxurious, because it had two rooms—one for sleeping, and one for everything else. It even had a covered porch out front, with a railing you could put your feet on. And the outhouse was only 10 paces away.

Juanita knew the Commander had a good record for harassing the enemy. This *could* be the perfect post. She walked ahead of Bevis and eyed the old woman on the porch. "Commander Shanahan?"

"Who wants to know?" The Commander peered around her propped-up feet and clutched mug.

"I'm Donna Wallace, and I ran into your Colonel Bevis

about seven miles due west of here. I've got messages from New Hampshire and several other commands. Can I talk to you for a few minutes?"

The Commander wished she hadn't just topped off dinner with eight ounces of corn whiskey. She made a brusque gesture toward the door.

The girl—no, it wasn't a girl, not a girl at all—walked past and inside, and Commander Bettina Shanahan followed and shut the door. "Welcome to Camp Ellaville."

"Thank you, Commander. The people in Laconia have a very, very high opinion of you."

"Because I do what we're *all* supposed to be doing. Kill the motherfuckers. Which gives you some idea of what a shitty job everybody else is doing." The Commander eased into a split hickory chair, and scrutinized the blonde. At least forty, and tough. "All right, let's have the messages."

"First, the visitor you expected is here."

A broad grin split the old woman's face, exposing the gaps in her teeth. "Heh, heh. I should have guessed. Heard about the California bus job, and poisoning that barracks in Memphis—"

"I get around."

"You do, you do indeed," the Commander cackled. Her WAC fatigues were much too big for her, and wrinkled. "Tell me why we in Ellaville have been honored with your presence. And would you like a drink?"

"A *drink*?"

"In the great Dixie tradition, we have been makin' our own." The Commander brandished a clumsily-blown glass jug filled with ominous fluid.

"Best offer I've had all day."

Of course, it was a trap, a ponderous practical joke. Newcomers usually gasped or coughed at their first swallow of the moonshine. Some even vomited. But this Juanita swallowed neatly and grinned. "Damn' fine booze!" Bettina refilled the camp-made pottery mug. "But let's get down to business."

"Right." Bettina poured herself another snort.

"Commander, the High Command has determined that the time for passive resistance by the United States Army is past. It is time for us to stop reacting, and start *acting* to drive these foreign invaders out of our country."

"How'd they figure that?"

"We *are* getting stronger. And they're getting weaker. You're kind of cut off down here..."

"Tell me about it," Bettina grunted. "Never even got the radio they promised."

"... but the tide *is* turning in our favor. It's time for us to step up harassment, weaken the occupation forces, take food, supplies, armaments, anything we can from them. And get ready for the uprising."

The Commander shifted in her chair. "Is there a timetable?"

"Sometime next year," Juanita lied.

"Nationwide?"

"No. We start in the East. Better supplies here, more people."

"Concentrating the effort—that's smart. What do you want Ellaville to do?"

"First, we've got to get you tied into the communications and supply network. Next messenger that comes along, we'll see to it you get your radio."

"Wish I knew what sonofabitch *did* get it." The old woman snorted grumpily. "We even tried to steal one from Valdosta."

Juanita riveted her disturbing eyes on Bettina. "How was it? What happened?"

"Nobody came back. Happens the same, every time we try to get a look at their setup." There was a knock on the cabin door. "Enter!" Bettina bawled.

Beauregard Bevis, who was Executive Officer of the Command, stuck his head around the door with mock servility. "Oh, uh, beg your pardon, ma'am..."

"Cut the crap, Bo. This here's the visitor we've been expecting."

He gaped. Surely the killer Juanita would be bigger, more menacing...he looked again at the eyes and knew. "My pleasure, uh..."

"Her rank's Brigadier General," the Commander growled. "And my name is Donna Wallace, for now."

"The Gen—Donna's been telling me we're to get ready for

a general rebellion." The Commander grabbed another clay mug from the table, and poured a shot for Bo.

"When?" His face was alight with joy.

"When we're ready, but within a year." Juanita braced her feet on the tabletop, and rocked her chair. "My orders are first, to secure the unit here. That means tightening up security, getting rid of leaks or spies. Two, send the High Command a complete assessment of the situation regionally—"

"Personnel? Supplies? Terrain?" Bo butted in.

"—together with a proposed plan of action. You ever tried stealing supplies from any of the Russkie outposts?"

"Sure. Sure." Bo scoffed. "It's not worth losing men for lousy AK-47's. How do we get the big stuff?"

"Lieutenant Colonel," Juanita rocked her chair forward and glared, "the High Command is not going to breach security by letting units fifteen hundred miles away know details months before they need to."

"Sorry."

She continued, mild again. "I can tell you, just among us, that a *full* range of weapons will be available for the uprising. But what's more important, what's completely up to us—will be overrunning and grabbing all the Russkie stuff we can without any support."

"And we have to let them know ahead of time what we can handle." Bo was getting excited again.

"Right. Uh—I would like to meet with you again in the morning. But right now," she gave a rueful grin, "I am one bushed chick. Where can I sleep?"

"My cabin," Bo said, and caught the Commander's devastating glare. "I'll sleep on the porch."

Rising from the rough-hewn chair, she seemed almost as old as the Commander. "Thanks...Bo, is it?"

"Beauregard Manigault Bevis." Bettina's voice dripped acid. "Several of the southland's finest families conspired to produce this rascal."

"Whom you regard as the son you never had." It was an old joke between them. "Donna, would you like something to eat?"

"Just sleep." Following him to the other cabin, across the clearing, she staggered.

* * *

There were birds, insects, and people going about their business. That much she established before figuring out what sound had waked her. It was a helicopter.

The camp froze, and anybody who was near the edge of the wooded area dove for cover. Juanita rolled off the bed and under it. Phoo! Cobwebs and dustballs. She held her nose, then sheepishly reckoned the copter was at least seven hundred feet above her, and not likely to hear one lousy sneeze. She let go of her nose and waited for the inevitable, which happened the moment Beauregard pushed the door open.

"Ahh-chew!"

"Bless you. Ma'am."

"Where's that chopper from? Christ, it's dirty under here," she added bitterly.

Bo thought she was being might dainty for a woman who traveled in bare feet and slept in her clothes. His drawl increased as his temper did. "Well, pardon my poor hospitality, ma'am, but my maid *and* my Hoover went bust at the same time."

"Cute. And the Katov?"

"How'd you . . . ?" He bit his tongue.

"Know it was a Katov? Practice, Colonel, practice. Those double rotors sound like scissors."

"You'll want breakfast. But, uh, the latrine's there." He pointed to the Commander's trim little outhouse.

"Is there any way . . ." She bit her lip. Was it possible she was embarrassed?

"What?"

"Any way I could get a bath?"

Bo gave her a big smile. She *was* human. "Well, of course there is, honey. You just stay right here, and I'll have them bring you everything."

In a few minutes, people appeared with an old copper tub, two threadbare towels marked "Rodeway Inns" and a cake of stern-looking yellow soap. In return, she gave them the sourballs and BBs she'd scavenged. After she washed herself in the tub, she washed her clothes. She wore a man's singlet undershirt of ribbed cotton, white cotton briefs whose elas-

15

tic was giving out, rolled-up Levis, a man's khaki shirt and her campaign jacket. They yielded a tubful of scum, so she wrapped Bevis's coverlet around her and went in search of rinse water.

"There a pump around here?" she asked an old black woman who was stirring an iron pot on a tripod. The woman looked her up and down, and pointed behind the Commander's house.

"Thanks."

She rinsed and wrung, rinsed and wrung out again. Hoping that nobody would rip off the possessions she'd hidden under the mattress, she carried her clothes back to the cabin in a dripping ball. Everything was still there. She eased into the wet clothes, packing her treasures—gun, knife, compass, garrote—back in her pockets. She was buttoning the shirt when Bevis knocked.

"Yo?" He looked annoyingly carefree, she decided. "The war going well, Lieutenant Colonel?"

"Oh, just smashingly well since you arrived on our humble scene, ma'am. And we—that is, the Commander, the council and I—wondered if you could spare us some of your expertise at a staff meeting?"

She was all business. Without a word, but trailed by dripping water, she marched to the Commander's cabin.

II

1.

Before the war, the United States military establishment would have laughed at the motley crew now serving as the Regional Command, United States Army.

But this was *after*. The likely candidates for the military—male, young and fit—were dead, in concentration camps, or conscript work cadres. Now the minorities, the disabled, and the women were in charge. Especially the women. Beside the Commander, the old woman who looked like Bette Davis, women were in charge of the Quartermaster's office, the Paymaster's office, and Medevac.

Intelligence was, the charge of a serious, weedy-looking young man whose lurching limp made his previous military exemption clear. The Medical Officer was a young man from India, as swarthy as all Bengal. He had been at Johns Hopkins on an exchange scholarship when the unthinkable happened. So much for his plans of a lucrative practice on Park Avenue, New York. Now it was vermin bites, fungi, and malnutrition he had to treat, just like home. If only he could get home.

"OK, staff conference in session," the Commander barked.

"Ma'am, our food situation is getting acute," the Quartermaster squalled.

"Our food situation is *always* acute," Bettina snapped back. "It's your job to relieve it."

The Quartermaster was bitter. "It isn't easy raising vegetables in the jungle."

"It'll be a lot less easy if the Russkies spot our gardens, and attack."

"And two of our cows are sick." This was the Quartermaster's serious news, and she'd been waiting to spring it. The

17

Commander's head swung toward the doctor, who raised his shoulders eloquently.

"One of them is simply old, I think. The other . . . some kind of intestinal parasite, perhaps."

"Slaughter the old one for meat," the old lady said briskly. "Take good care of the other one. Maybe she'll pull through. Next?"

"Reporting an increase in Russkie overflights," Intelligence said.

"How much increase?"

Intelligence peered at the scrap of paper, wishing his glasses hadn't been smashed in the escape from Memphis. "From an average of two or three a week over the last three months, to eleven in the last ten days." Everybody but the strange blonde in the corner stirred uneasily.

"One flew over yesterday, at dusk," somebody said.

"And it circled."

The Commander rapped on the table. "Intelligence, any other signs of increased enemy activity?" She knew it was important to keep Staff meetings disciplined, from her thirty years in the WACs.

"To the best of our knowledge, they have not pinpointed our location yet."

The Commander snorted.

"What do these choppers look like?" the strange blonde asked. The room tittered at her naiveté.

"I should introduce Donna Wallace, who's come to us from New Hampshire," the Commander said. The chuckles stopped. "Look like?"

"The one came over this morning was a Katov—Ka-25. Double rotors. They've got some of them equipped with high-altitude cameras, infrared scanners, radar—stuff like that. You see any?"

"You mean, they could see us *through* the trees?" the Paymaster bleated. The blonde gave her a look of open contempt.

"It's possible they're just taking radiation readings," the Commander frowned at the rough wood table.

"Bullshit." The blonde spoke flatly. "Even if they are, when they find out it's not hot here, they'll come in. If they *do* see

18

you, they'll come in to get you." The Staff inhaled collectively. The Commander knew it was time to take charge.

"Donna has seen more than we have, isolated here in Florida. I want the camp put on twenty-four hour alert, with a complete security cordon. If that means stopping other activities, do it. Quartermaster?"

"Yes, ma'am." The Quartermaster's petulance was gone.

"Prepare a contingency plan for evacuating the camp with maximum speed and minimum loss of supplies."

"And make it fast." The Staff didn't know who this Donna was, but she had to swing a lot of weight to get the last word on their Commander. The conference broke up rapidly.

The Commander, the Exec, and Juanita bent over a rumpled and ragged Exxon touring map of Florida. Juanita's scarred but immaculate forefinger traced a line from Mobile, north of Pensacola. "The trains run here, headed for Tallahassee, so we know that's cold."

"The question is, where do they think it's hot?"

"Presumably, they *know* it's hot where they dropped the nukes," Bettina snarled at Bo.

"But now, but now..." Juanita was looking at the map with dreamy eyes, "they are doing a little probing here, a little testing there—and finding out that some of the C-zones aren't hot any more. If they ever were."

"Why would they care about a little bitty strip of land?"

"They purely love good farm land, that I know." Bettina sounded resigned.

"Maybe they want to send Florida fruit baskets home to the folks."

"They want us all dead," Juanita said flatly. "Or slaves. Face it. Hell, they probably want the fruit baskets, too. Since California's no good." They looked at her, and she responded. "Hotter than the hinges of hell." They absorbed it for a minute, all that golden land, the dream state—now damnation country.

"What happened..." The Commander bit her tongue.

"What happened where?" There seemed to be softness in Juanita's tone. "Your home?"

"Lawrence, Kansas. Between Topeka and Kansas City."

"Kansas City's gone," Juanita said with a blank face. "The C-zone—Lawrence is near Olathe? Well, then. It's in the zone. And that's no phony zone."

"Thank you, General." The Commander was iron.

"How fast can you pull out?"

"How fast do we have to?"

Bo butted in. "*Do* we have to?"

"Fucking-A. Look, the Russkie soldiers are scared shitless of radiation. They wouldn't be nosing around here if they didn't know it's safe. They know it's cold, and they know you're here. Where's their base?"

"We figure they came from Valdosta. None of the outposts have copters. That we know of."

"If it was me," the newcomer dragged her thumb and forefinger around the corners of her mouth, "I'd haul ass right now."

"Where to?"

"Where does it *really* get hot?"

The Commander and the Exec gaped at each other. "You want us to go into a *real* C-zone?"

"You want to get wiped out *now*, by the Russkies, or take your chances?" she challenged.

"There's a couple here that refugeed from Alachua." The Commander stabbed the map with a stubby thumb. "They saw the flash when Gainesville went up. Did they say about damage?"

"Seems to me," Bo scratched his chin, "they just lost their windows and all. They said something about seeing the firestorm that night, but they were already north of Alachua."

"OK, agreed, Gainesville really *is* hot." Juanita was businesslike about the apocalypse. "They probably wouldn't bother with anything due west toward the Gulf..."

"Or east." The Commander didn't see any likely targets on the right-hand side of the map.

"So let's say she gets mildly hot somewhere between High Springs and... hey, I'd like to talk to these folks from Alachua?" The tone was questioning, the command unmistakable. Bo stepped out on the porch and muttered to the guard.

* * *
20

Ed and Doris Kelly's retirement ended when the flash blew in the louvered glass windows on their patio facing south. Ed still had trouble with his eyes, because he'd been on the patio, reading the N.A.A.R.P. newsletter. Now Ed and Doris wore torn, baggy military castoffs, put in their dentures only for meals, and felt better than they had in years.

"You wanted to see us, Ma'am?" Ed stepped smartly into the Commander's cabin, squinting at the unaccustomed brilliance of a kerosene lamp. Doris combed her hair with her fingers.

"Sit down, folks." The Commander waved toward the bench by the wall. "This here's Donna Wallace; she's just come from New Hampshire." Ed and Doris looked obediently at the skinny blonde with the burned-out eyes.

"You're from Alachua? Tell me about it."

They didn't ask what It was. "It was between five-thirty and six that night. The local news was on the TV. The sun was setting, but we had the lights on, and Doris was in the kitchen, cooking."

"You were facing south?"

"Not right south. The TV was over on the west side, and I was catty-corner to it, reading. Then the sky went white, and everything went off, and Doris yelled at me to get down and shut my eyes."

"You knew right away what it was?"

"Certainly!" Doris Kelly considered herself nobody's fool. "I got Ed into the kitchen, 'cause he couldn't see, and in a couple minutes the blast came and knocked everything to smithereens."

"How long before you could see again, Ed?"

"Oh, things started coming in like overexposed film in a couple hours. Still have to wear my dark glasses in the sunlight."

"When did you get out of there?" The blonde was eyeing them intently.

"I always insisted we have emergency kits packed for tornadoes or hurricanes," Doris said in a businesslike tone. "Ed wanted to take the car, but I said 'Anybody that can move will be on the roads.' Sitting ducks, they were."

"We just grabbed our kits and radio, and hightailed it for the woods. Made it north past High Springs that night." Ed saw the three at the table check their map. "And near to Fort White the next day. Dirt roads all the way."

"What they want to know, Ed," Doris nudged him, "is did we ever have the sickness."

"No, no symptoms. Still got all our hair and skin."

"We met a young mama from Waldo, though. Remember?" The Kellys looked sad. "She had a little bitty girl in the worst way, and she was sick, too."

"Didn't get out as fast as we did," Ed concluded.

"Ever see anybody else with the sickness?" The Wallace woman was pretending to be vague, Doris could tell.

"We heard—to tell the truth, we *smelled* a lot of death on the road. Minute we saw buzzards, though, I told Ed I wasn't going thataway, any time."

"And you came right up here?"

"And stayed right here until we ran into a bunch of Loyalists."

The blonde gave a nod of dismissal. "Thank you, Ed and Doris," the Commander said, and they went back across the clearing to the hut they'd built of logs and mud.

"Jesus, were *they* lucky." Juanita was grim as she looked at the map again. "The wind here must have blown the dust every way but north, or they'd be goners."

"Right after the war, I remember," Bo mused, "we had a little storm, like. Blew right off the Gulf for eight, ten days maybe."

"So that's why the Atlantic tuna glow in the dark," Juanita said sourly. Bo laughed. They looked at the map awhile longer, and the Commander decided to move out the next afternoon. But that was too late.

2.

Juanita insisted *she* sleep on the porch, so Bo could have his bed again. He was surprised to see she'd washed the tattered sheets and coverlet, and spread them neatly over the rotting foam-rubber mattress. He snuffed out the candles while she was still staring out at the compound, her back propped against the log wall.

Camp lore held that these sharecropper's cabins had been a criminal hideout, for men on the run from the local prisons and correctional farms. And a country brothel, too. There had never been any electricity or water lines—no traces the Russkies could find on a survey map. Still, she felt uneasy.

Deciding that semi-suffocation was preferable to being eaten alive by Florida mosquitoes, she tucked the tarpaulin firmly under her, all around from toes to scalp, and fell instantly asleep.

Something was wrong. She knew it before she could remember where she was, who she was supposed to be. She pulled the tarp clear of her ears and—they were out there. With feral silence, she freed her whole body, and slipped through the broken screen door. Bo tried to say "What?" but a hand on his mouth and something hard jammed into his larynx stopped him.

"They're advancing on us," the woman hissed. "What's your alarm signal? Which way do we evacuate?" The hand and the gun barrel slid away.

"Signal is this," he held up a birdcall whistle. "Five times. Only plan we ever had was head south."

"Give the signal. I'll get the Commander."

"You sure about this? I don't hear anything." Juanita froze, and he could see those unnatural eyes glaring at him. Talk about glowing in the dark. He grabbed the birdcall on the chain around his neck, and leapt out to the porch. He blew five times, paused, then five times more.

There were rustles and moans and sighs. Somebody was stupid enough to light a torch, and the firing began.

Please God, let them have no tanks, nothing heavy! Juanita cried inside. Guided by the flashes of gunfire, she dodged and slithered to the Commander's cabin. Oozing up the steps, she saw the old woman's bare feet, and looked up to see Bettina positioning an M-16 to fire. She sprang, poised with one arm to grab the barrel, one to knock Bettina down.

It was no contest, even if the Commander did know judo.

Juanita sat stride her, muzzling her. She leaned down until their noses were an inch apart. "Bettina! Asshole! You're too valuable to waste."

She saw the fire in the old woman's eyes subside, and took her hand away. "Any idea where to rendezvous?"

"Twenty miles due south. Town of Mayo. There was a new shopping center, had a big basement garage. I think it's still OK." The Commander gasped, realizing just how strong this zombie was.

"You go. I'll tell them." Juanita vaulted over the porch railing one-handed, like a man. The Commander grabbed her gun, ammo pack, and knapsack, and headed out the back door as a starshell cruelly illiminated the Ellaville camp.

Juanita collided with Bo, galloping toward headquarters. "She's moving out."

"Where?"

"Mayo. Twenty miles south, straight down. Meet in the basement garage of the shopping center."

Basement garage? In Florida? No time to ask. Bo reversed direction and made a wide arc around the communal field. He saw Juanita head around the other way.

The heavy foliage and disorganization of the camp prevented the Russians from a proper attack with the first star shell. But the second flare, and the third, improved their aim, and the real killing began.

When he saw no more living Americans to tell, Bo dove into the bush, and headed away from the Russian fire. He hoped that was due south, but didn't really care. The time just before dawn was the hardest part. As at dusk, the half-and-half light tricked your eyes. He was feeling the bush with his hands, like a blind man, looking for the sunrise to act as his compass. Immediate terror past, he found each step agony. Fronds and tendrils grabbed for his face in an oily way. Gooey leaves and roots snared his feet.

When he got a fix on the rising sun, he was set to collapse on the festering ground.

Until he heard the explosions behind him.

The goddamned Russkies were bombing the camp! Adrenalin surged, and he pushed briskly forward. South.

* * *

Sigmund Wallberg had been mightily vexed when he got the ruling from the Zoning Commission. No parking lot! Were they crazy, or just out to get him?

Jerry Allcott, Town Supervisor, gave him a baroquely evasive story. "Sigmund, we've got a real boom here on our hands, as I'm sure you know." Jerry snickered, alluding to the half-million everybody knew Sigmund had made on the Interstate deal.

"So?"

"So we have an obligation not to destroy the character of our town with unplanned, uncontrolled development." Jerry was marvelously smug.

"And you consider a shopping center—a shopping center like every other—progressive—town in America has—to be uncontrolled?" Sigmund was pretty uncontrolled, himself.

"Sigmund, we've got a drive-in food place on one side of your lot, a golf course on the north, and, I must tell you . . ." Jerry leafed through his accordion folder ". . . to the west, a major national construction firm has filed plans for a condominium townhouse development. Which would mean a fence right on two edges of your property."

"So," Sigmund roared, as much as a Viennese *could* roar, "my shopping center has no place for shoppers to park? Is that it?"

Jerry raised a cautionary forefinger. "Ah, ah, ah," he tutted. "We simply suggest that you borrow a tip or two from our northern cousins."

"Hanh?"

"And build your parking space *under* the mall."

Sigmund gaped. An underground edifice? On swampy Florida land? He would have to waterproof the cement walls eight ways from Sunday. He would have to reinforce the walls in ways even NASA hadn't dreamed of. Sump pumps. Drainage channels. A dark suspicion that Jerry Allcott had connections in the concrete industry. Sigmund felt a headache coming on.

But now, some years later, Sigmund felt quite differently about his parking garage. He and his wife were living in it.

* * *

The first party of Loyalists that arrived stood suspiciously at the edge of the swamp (where the condos would have been) and stared. The place was too big, too new, too whole for the Russkies to have left it alone. Wasn't it?

Right after the war had started, looters cleaned out the Grand Union, Dart Drug, Belk's Department Store, and Pic 'n' Pay Liquors. The few who stayed in Mayo went over the Singer Sewing Center, Suncoast Hardware, and Diana's Band Box at their leisure.

Sigmund and Helga Wallberg had set up housekeeping on the top parking level, in the men's room. They had a nice supply of canned and dried goods stacked in the last three stalls. they got water from the self-propelled artesian well bored to water the lawns of the mall. It tasted foul, but they didn't notice. Sigmund ran a hose from just inside the garage door to their quarters, so they could cook and bathe with ease.

The parties of goons and looters, from the edges of bombed cities, had stopped coming through some time ago. Dead of radiation, the Wallbergs guessed. So Sigmund left the garage door open, instead of cranking it down. His wife heard the patter of bare feet first. She locked the door of the men's room, then stepped gingerly on two cases of canned corn to look out the slit of a window.

It looked like an army! A ragtag army, to be sure, but some of them were wearing American uniforms, and she thought she heard American speech.

Sigmund's tap-code sounded on the door.

"It's Americans!" Helga was thrilled.

"It's *trouble!*" He was furious. "They have guns and all. The invaders will follow." Sigmund re-bolted the door behind him.

Helga Wallberg had spent the best part of her adult life doing as Sigmund told her. But this was too much. She squared her scrawny shoulders. "Sigmund, they are *our* people, and I am going to help them!" She made a futile pass at grooming her gray, wispy hair, and unlocked the door.

The Commander arrived in time to see the remainder of her troops using bayonets, axes and hammers to open a store of canned food. Libby's. Broadcast. Conte. Green Giant. She thought for a moment that she was hallucinating, until a one-armed man thrust an opened can of corned beef hash under her nose.

"Commander! People here living in the basement!"

Bettina controlled herself long enough to bark "Bring them to me," and dug into the hash with hooked fingers. The woman was eager, co-operative. She had led them to the food, the guard explained. The man was something else.

"Identify yourselves."

"And what about *you*?" he glared.

"I am Commander Shanahan, United States Army. We mostly call ourselves Loyalists. The Russians caught us at Ellaville. Where did you get all this food?" She saw the woman Juanita slip into the circle around them as she spoke.

"We were here in the building when the bombing started," Helga said haltingly. "My husband," she waved at the truculent Sigmund, "figured out right away what was going on. We got the food from the Grand Union, and hid it."

"I built this!" Sigmund waved a hortatory arm at the moss-covered concrete. "We live here. You have taken all our food!"

"Tough shit." Juanita's drawl carried clearly, and the crowd howled with laughter. "Now you can starve like the rest of us. Seen any Russkies? Any planes or copters go over?"

"We hear, sometimes, a jet plane," Helga spoke reflectively. "I don't remember hearing any helicopters. And Russian soldiers—never."

"Anybody else left in this town?"

Sigmund spat. "Fools!"

"Oh, yes, there are the Andersons in the citrus grove," Helga offered. "And that nice black family by the river. We spoke, oh, a month ago."

"You mean," the Commander put down the empty tin can, and looked fierce, "you mean, you don't *know* who's left alive around here? You haven't gone out and made an effort to help them?"

"Why should we?" Sigmund was contemptuous. From the crowd came a long, loud raspberry. Helga hung her head.

After everybody was inside the garage and guards mounted, the Commander sent for the Exec and Juanita. They found Bettina Shanahan propped against a damp concrete wall, looking a generation older than the day before. "Thank you for saving my life," she said to Juanita. "Now, do we stay here?"

"It must—we must be getting near the hot zone," Bo said uneasily. The Commander knew he was even more terrified of radiation sickness than most. He had seen a field of people dying, east of Tampa.

"No."

"How do you know?"

"No bodies lying around. Skeletons," Juanita said flatly. "Where the radiation was bad enough it's still hot, they died on the road."

"Thanks a lot." Bo was bitter. "You're saying, if the radiation isn't enough to kill you in your tracks, you don't consider it hot?"

Juanita was squatting, and she leaned forward. "Colonel, I have talked to military men and nuclear scientists about this. They say, after all these years, the borderline, the windblown stuff is *gone*."

"Only direct target areas would still be hot?" the Commander mused.

"Within the radius of visible blast damage, or in areas where wildlife—particularly rodents and small mammalia— are absent." Juanita recited by rote from some dread text.

"But the Russians must know that, too."

"Let's stop kidding ourselves." Juanita's eyes drilled both of them. "We have to go further south, far enough so the Russkies will be afraid to follow. That's the only way we'll live, for now. We should take the Suwannee down to the Gulf, then head for the Withlacoochee. And if that isn't far enough, keep going."

Juanita wasn't only right, she was a superior officer. "We'll leave in the afternoon." It would be cooler then, and everybody could get some sleep.

3.

The ragtag army marched—or limped—south on orders. Helga Wallberg followed, and the enraged Sigmund followed her. The scouts picked up the black family Helga knew, and the Andersons decided to stay put, but told the Commander the Americans were free to harvest the grapefruit and orange in their overgrown groves.

The offer was superfluous, as all the trees had been stripped bare by the time it was made.

"Was it Clausewitz who said 'an army marches on its stomach'?" The Commander trudged with the slow, steady step of a veteran.

"Napoleon," Beauregard answered. At least a military education was still worth something.

Buoyed by yesterday's orgy of food, the Loyalists made good time. Some who couldn't walk—from injuries, handicaps or age—were pulled on homemade wagons, bicycle rigs and sledges. The Command decided to take a chance and follow the highway south. It was so easy to traverse, nobody complained about traveling at night. In the daytime, they slept in the culverts and drank from the storm drains.

Juanita was impressed by the number of followers they were picking up en route.

The Commander was not. Down here, these people were completely out of touch. They were well-fed, feisty, and frustrated by their lack of opportunities to revenge themselves on the enemy. All they'd had to do was survive in a tropical climate that gave them fruit, fish, wild meat, and water. "They don't know the Russkies, don't know reality. They're just overjoyed to be in touch with America again."

When they'd been marching five and a half days, they were in sight of an inland lake, with a river leading in and out of it, east to west.

Bettina planted her feet, and made a pronouncement loud enough for the whole camp to hear.

"You want to know 'where the hell are we?'" The camp became still, even eating their meager, hand-trapped meat quietly. "We are on the north shore of Lake Rousseau, which is formed by the Withlacoochee River, somewhere between the towns of Inglis," she pointed to her right, west, "and Dunellon." She pointed east. "We *hope* we are far enough south, far enough inside what the Russkies call the zone, to be safe. But we don't know; nobody knows."

When they were strafed by Russkie planes, three days later, Juanita knew. Knew there was a traitor in camp.

"Oh, shit," Bo kept shaking his head.

"I was afraid of this." Bettina was almost as calm as the General. "We keep picking up people, trusting they are what they claim . . ."

Juanita sneered. "Bullshit. It's probably somebody's been here all along. Somebody you trust. Only the Russkies just decided to put the screws on the guy now, and nail you. Us."

The Commander and Exec protested vigorously.

"Doesn't matter," Juanita waved them away. "I'll find him, her, whatever. You just tell the camp," she pondered a minute, "tell them there *was* a traitor in our midst, but we got 'em."

"What?" Bo yelped.

"Good plan," Bettina rocked back on her heels and stared at the feeble fire.

The camp was speedily taking on permanent characteristics. Scavenging was good. There were derelict rowboats to fish from, game in the forest, fruit trees in quantity, and abandoned houses to be dismantled. In three days, huts and tents sprang up, spotted throughout the brush, as they'd learned at Ellaville. There were proper latrines, covered stone cooking pits, and bathing spots on the river bank.

The Intelligence Officer approached the Commander's tent to make his daily report. Juanita followed.

"Good morning, ma'am!" He saluted briskly with his cane, and stepped inside. Juanita was inches behind, and her gun touched his right temple. Without a word, she untied the tent flap, pushed the cripple forward, and closed the canvas.

"Here's our leak."

"Nonsense! This man has been with us since . . ." the Commander trailed off, feeling foolish. It was just like the bitch had said. Somebody who was an old friend, from the inner circle.

Juanita put her mouth close to the man's ear, and whispered so only those in the tent could hear. "His wife is in Valdosta, isn't she?" Intelligence nodded, miserably. "And he didn't know it until they let him see her in the compound. The concentration camp."

Juanita raised her eyes from Intelligence to the Commander. "All he wants now is to get back to Valdosta, so he can try to save his wife before the Russkies find out he's of no more use to them."

Bettina was nonplussed. It was a human, righteous solution, but not like Juanita. "We need assurances," she grumbled.

Intelligence looked even more miserable.

"This man wishes us no harm" the blonde said smoothly, but her gun was still in place. "Once we move on, his knowledge is useless. Why not give him the chance to save his wife—and himself?"

Bettina's brain whirled for a moment. She made a brusque gesture of dismissal. Juanita pocketed her gun, opened the tent flap. "C'mon," she said softly and put a gentle hand on the arm that didn't use the cane.

A giant weight was lifted from Intelligence's chest. He could free himself of the guilt, now. This woman—she called herself Donna Wallace, but she was obviously much too important to be an unknown. Maybe even the legendary Juanita? Although he had always imagined that Juanita must be some kind of Latina. This woman had discovered the trap they had him in.

She could have him killed. But she spoke true. What more harm could he do, now? He would make his painful, gimpy way north. When he met the Russian patrols, he'd tell them to take him to Captain Muzoyev, in Valdosta. Then, somehow . . . he would get to see Bonnie.

They were at the edge of the swamp. There was muddy water, and a rowboat. "What?"

"For security." The woman unwrapped the coarse rope tying the boat to a knotty cypress tree. "We'll get you a few

31

miles away, by swamp, and we'll hightail it out of here by the time you figure out which way's north." Her smile was ironic, sympathetic.

His legs might not work well, but he could row. The woman pointed out obstacles in their path, navigating by some instinct until they were too far in the swamp for him to have any idea of their location. Then she looked bewildered. "Oh, shit. I could have sworn..."

He stopped rowing. "What's the matter?"

"There's supposed to be an old pier there." She pointed behind him, and he turned on his bench to look.

One arm held his shoulders, the other grabbled his head and twisted the opposite way. Before his neck and brain stem snapped, he thought he'd seen the Angel of Death.

An hour later, Bo watched the rowboat splash through the swamp grass to camp. It banged gracelessly into firm land, and the rower climbed out. She dragged the aluminum shell onto dry, high land.

"You took him out where he'd get lost?" Bo asked.

"Killed the fucker, and dumped him in the swamp." Juanita brushed the palms of her hands against her thighs, and walked away.

III

1.

"There should have been somebody by now." Juanita paced restlessly around the Commander's fire. "I got here in—April?"

"You sure?"

"No." She was rueful. "Somewhere around there. Has anybody here been keeping a calendar?"

As luck would have it, the truculent Sigmund Wallberg was stickler for days, dates, and hours. "It's the fourteenth of August," he growled, hunched over a dinner of stewed armadillo. "Who wants to know?"

"God. He's lost his calendar watch," the Exec snarled back, and stalked away.

"Four months. There should have *been* a courier by now. Maybe they got caught in the Ellaville ambush."

"Maybe they can't find our new camp." Bo picked up his dish of stew. Its aluminum depths had once held a frozen pot pie, he could tell, and his stomach yearned for the past.

"Well, better go contact somebody." Juanita was eating from a foam-plastic dish, and she gave it a final lick.

"Where? Who?"

"There is—or was—a Loyalist camp on the Tennessee-North Carolina border." Juanita's spoon handle traced a quick outline in the dirt, a geographic skill Bo envied. "Right between Asheville and Knoxville. It's cold there. Just too damn rugged for the Russkies to take it on. They've got a radio, they're wired in. I don't know anyplace nearer to find out what's going on—and get a message north."

"You're not going without me."

The Commander had been silent, but now she yelled at Bo, "No way!" Juanita just stared.

33

"What if she gets killed?" Bo shrilled back at the old lady, waving a casual thumb at Juanita. "We're screwed. What if the High Command decides she should go someplace else?"

"Ahh," Bettina grumbled. "We're screwed. Can't send somebody *alone* on a mission like this. If I had my way, I'd send a whole squad. I know, I know..." she fended off their protests. "You're the ones that go. Both of you. General..." She found it difficult to look the woman directly in the eye, but she did.

"General, you owe us that much. Some backup for you in case..."

"OK. In case."

"Now," Bettina said brusquely, "what do I do for a temporary Executive Officer?"

"Myron Jackson," Bo said, and nobody blinked an eye. Bo thought how everything had changed, because his family owned a plantation, back in his former life, and Myron Jackson was black.

Myron had been in the Marine Corps, in what he referred to as "the Nam." Myron had been "serving time," as he said, trying to enlist semi-literate youngsters from the slums of Tampa in the Marine Corps, when the war came. Myron had quickly and prudently removed hiself to a cabin he knew of, in the swamps, and remained there until he heard of a U.S. Army detachment in the area.

Myron had arrived in camp with a kit bag full of immaculate Marine Corporal uniforms. He was a martinet, and a born leader, and the General, Commander and Exec knew it.

"OK," Bettina said.

"And your Quartermaster sucks." Juanita was already slipping away into the woods, but she looked back. "That Wallberg guy is a prick, but he'd do the job."

Bo followed her into the shadows. Bettina rocked back and forth on her haunches and wondered how a zombie could be such a good judge of character.

When relieved of her duties, the ex-Quartermaster whined with relief.

Sigmund Wallberg was no more gracious, when told of his elevation. He muttered darkly about "parasites—bloodsuckers—goldbrickers," and immediately began to organize the camp's supply system. By the time Juanita and Bo were far enough north to see signs of the occupying power, Sigmund was ordering seven able-bodied children and a great-grandmother to make snares for quail.

No question. They had gotten out of Ellaville just in time. Now the Russkies were in force on a line east-west from Gainesville. Bo and Juanita had to travel by night. There were so many overlapping groups of the occupying forces, they could hear strange commands hailing each other by bullhorn.

"Christ, how can there be so *many*?" Bo said bitterly.

"They're spread out pretty thin. They've got jeeps and armored personnel carriers, but nothing big. No troop trains running. Yet."

"How do we get through?"

"You mean *where* do we get through." Juanita's eyes gleamed, and Bo knew he was doomed to travel through a *real* C-zone.

They slipped furtively east along the pulsating lines of the occupation. One night's march later, the Russkie lines seemed to be interrupted, then sporadic, then gone. Then came the signs he'd only heard about. Their paint was peeling in the tropical climate, and some were being consumed by rot and termites. They showed the three black propellors on the chrome yellow background. He couldn't read the top line, but the bottom said CAUTION! RADIOACTIVE AREA!

The woman was grinning at him. "Want to say a rosary?"

"I want to go home to my mommy. But, barring that—" he strode past the sign.

Now their traveling was much easier. If you could keep from thinking *why*, he reminded himself. Heading due north, they saw the signs sometimes to their left, sometimes to their right.

"How far north?"

"Until we clear Jacksonville."

He plodded along dutifully, trying to reconstruct a map in his head. Just north of Jacksonville was—"Oh, Christ. We are headed straight for the Okefenokee Swamp," he moaned. "Coral snakes. Gators. Bloodsuckers."

"Cheer up," she was sarcastic. "It'll probably be typhoid or malaria that kills us." Juanita marched ahead briskly, or as briskly as one could move through tangled undergrowth.

The Okefenokee was a piece of cake. They found an algae-covered fiberglass boat, anchored by its rusting outboard motor. When the motor was dumped, the boat was light enough to pole along the swamp channels. They could even take turns sleeping as they traveled.

The next day, he woke up when she said, "Wow." She was pulling Spanish moss out of her eyes, and staring ahead, nonplussed.

It was a scene from the past. It had to be a time warp, or the Twilight Zone.

There was a mobile home—bright yellow and white—with little aluminum awnings.

It was up on concrete blocks, and there were folding chairs and a barbecue grill to complete the picture. Parked snugly alongside was a pearly gray Buick Riviera. The grass was trimmed, there was a TV antenna and two small, black French poodles barked at their arrival.

Juanita and Bo stared. At the scene, then at each other.

A gruff command came from the trailer, to still the dogs. An old man in a flowered sport shirt and checked shorts got out, followed by an old woman in a Lane Bryant nylon jersey shirtwaist. They stared at the couple in the boat, who stared back.

"Hello there!" the old man said jovially.

"Hello! Hellooo!" Bo was wildly relieved to hear English. "Who're you folks?"

"Who are *you*?" the old man asked the swarthy young man in the tattered American uniform, and the blonde girl with the gun.

"Oh, uh, I'm Beauregard Bevis, Lieutenant Colonel, United States Air Force..." Juanita looked at him sharply, "and this is Donna Wallace; she's working for the American forces."

"Well, come in! Come in!" the old woman waved. "You folks had your breakfast yet?"

Nora and Don Polletti hailed from Worcester, Massachusetts.

They were on a trailer trip the winter of the war, looking at land for their retirement in Florida. Driving through the Okefenokee, they decided to cheat a little bit. The sign said "Camping Site" but there was no one else, so they parked their trailer. The next morning, there were jet plane sounds and explosions that rocked the ground. Their radio made funny noises, then silence. Three days later, they began to hear a language they took to be Russian on the channels. They started fishing and trapping for food, and roamed around the swamp.

"Then we found it. The Ranger headquarters."

"And?" Bo prompted.

"Them Park Rangers musta *known* World War Three was coming," Don said stoutly. "Enough canned and dried food to feed an army, and so much gas the Ay-rabs'd be jealous."

"That's how we live," Nora said. "We use the gas to run the car engine. For e-lectricity. And we eat the food."

Bo and Juanita pondered the perfection of it all. "Ever see anybody else?"

"A few have come through. They tell us this is supposed to be a radioactive area, but we're OK."

"And we don't plan on any kids at *this* stage in life!" Nora giggled.

Don raised his hand. "It's like the Lord said—the Day of Judgment is at hand, and the righteous shall come through the flames and thunder and trembling of the Earth..."

Nora finished the litany. "And they shall be whole of flesh, and rejoice. You folks ever seriously considered the faith of the Seventh Day Adventist Church?"

"Sure steered us right." Don was serene.

"These people that come through," Juanita said. She was eyeing the Pollettis warily. "What else they say?"

"Oh, some have been fleeing south, into the con-tam-i-nated zone. And some have been sneakin' north, to fight or something. Hasn't come to much."

"Why do you say that?"

"Because the Lord says this shall be our time of trial and tears."

"And because they're still begging on the radio for more Americans to join them," Nora added more practically.

"Radio?" the visitors gaped.

"Sure. Didn't you know?" Don was matter-of-fact now. "There's American radio coming from someplace called Tara. Only broadcasts from time to time, calling for people to fight, talking about the invaders and the uprising." He saw their faces glow. "You folks have anything to do with—"

"Yes," Bo said curtly. "This is very important, Don. Tell us *everything* this Tara radio says."

"Well . . . they don't say where they broadcast from. They don't say when they'll be coming on again. Sometimes the signal's weak. But they say they are, uh, 'gathering strength for the day we shall rise' uh, and throw the ungodly invaders out.'"

"They tell about atrocities the godless have committed," Nora added primly. "What shall I cook for supper?"

Slurping up Dinty Moore Beef Stew and warm Hi-C, Bo thought he was in a dream. The Pollettis were telling about a nationwide network of forces, a master plan, a guerrilla force that would re-establish their nation. He had not thought he would live long enough to see it. Deep down, he had to admit to himself, he hadn't believed Juanita. While their hosts fussed over the Sterno stove, he whispered to her. "Still want to head for Asheville?"

"This Tara sounds legit," she said cautiously, and gave the Pollettis a glibly warm smile. "Where is it they say we should report?"

"Never said. Just the name Tara."

"I think it's bedtime, now." Nora was rather like a house mother. Bo felt vaguely uneasy about being in the company of a woman not his wife.

"We . . . uh, we'll not bother you." He began to back clumsily out of the trailer.

"You just stretch out on those chaise longues . . ." Nora pronounced it "Chase Lounges" " . . and put these over you." She thrust a pair of dog-eared, yellow thermal blankets at them. "Sorry I can't offer you toothpaste, but *that* ran out some time ago. We use the baking soda you'll find by the water tap."

Silently, Bo and Juanita prepared their beds, the best either had rested on since they could remember. He went to relieve himself in the bushes, and Juanita began to clean her teeth with baking soda and her right forefinger. She heard hasty blundering through the bush.

Bo lurched into the clearing. "Scarlett O'Hara from Tara!" he almost yelled. "It's got to be—this Tara's got to be— someplace from *Gone With the Wind!*"

Juanita nodded, and then began to snicker. Bo's fly was still open, and his penis hung out.

2.

In the morning, they found Texaco road maps in the glove compartment of the Buick. Scarlett's Tara was somewhere near Atlanta, they remembered.

"Which direction?" Bo muttered. "I'm trying to picture Vivien Leigh and Clark Gable . . ."

"Didn't you read the *book*?" Juanita whispered furiously.

"Nope." His finger started a circle northwest of the city. "Chamblee. Stone Mountain."

"That was in it, Stone Mountain. A big battle, near the end of the Civil War."

He fixed her with a fishy eye. "War Between the States, *if* you please. Conyers . . . Stockbridge . . . Jonesboro." Juanita's hands grabbed his wrist so hard it hurt.

"That was the . . . county seat in the book." She stuck her finger down beside his. "Lovejoy . . . Fayetteville! Scarlett went to school in Fayetteville."

"You *memorized* that book?" He could see she was ready to hit the road. "We should give these people something. The Pollettis." She looked blank, lost in speculation. "I'll get some fish." He walked toward the swampy water's edge, pulling his fishline and hook out of a back pocket.

Three catfish later, he gave in to the silently pacing figure, and proffered his catch to their hosts, with thanks. By the time he'd reached the "hope to see you again" stage, she had already plunged into the brush.

It was drier, heading north. They were aiming for Waycross, or its ruins, and from there they planned to ease northwest. They had two hundred miles to cover to hit the southern suburbs of Atlanta. "Jeez, you'd think it would be hot *there*."

"Which makes it a good place to hide out." Juanita spoke curtly. She was trying to find the right way to tell him she'd stolen six cans of anchovies from the Pollettis. They were thin, and easy to hide in her jacket.

Explanations were not necessary. That night, they ran into the occupying power. No big forts or encampments. Not an air strip. The Russians were just living there, running lumber mills. Mills that used conscript Americans for labor.

He hadn't seen it before, because he hadn't left the C-zone. The wooden stockades, barbed wire, and searchlights left him speechless. "What do you *think* it is, asshole?" she demanded. "What do you think you're fighting?"

The fence ran around the feet of four small mountains. The mill was down on the river in the valley that passed between them. From the top of one mountain, they could see the army of workers, dressed in drab brown uniforms. They could see the guards, too, with their Kalashnikovs. They were in gun towers, and they controlled the searchlights. The mill seemed to run around the clock. The lumber floated down the river to the sea, at St. Andrew's Sound, she explained. There it could be loaded on ships and taken to Russia. Or anyplace.

He found himself choking. "Degrading, isn't it?" she jeered. "You should see the way they're running the mines in Pennsylvania. Or the rice paddies in Louisiana, with children. *Our* children. If you really want to get sick, that is." Most of the time she was unemotional, like the dead. He was astounded at the flash of humanity.

"Let's . . . get away from this. I want to sleep." He staggered a few more miles through pine scrub and gone-to-wilderness farms. When they fell down on the ground, she slapped something cold and flat and rectangular in his hand, without a word. He fell asleep instantly.

Anchovies? What the hell was a tin of Star of the Sea Anchovies (St. Michael's, Maryland) doing in his hand? She was already up, studying the map she'd stolen from the Pollettis. Christ, that, too! But the concept of anchovies sounded pretty good, even though he knew they'd leave him thirsty.

"What's the word?"

"Fucking tourist maps," she said bitterly. "Never tell you

where the military targets would be. What I'd give for one really up-to-date..."

"Up-to-occupation, you mean." He decided he could dish it out, too. "Surely the great Juanita knows where every Russian..." He trailed off because she had a truly malevolent glare. She pulled the battered compass out of her pocket, and he realized he'd never seen her with any kind of female accoutrement. Not even a comb. Nor, his thoughts trod gingerly, anything for the, uh, female cycle. He pulled his six-inch Ace comb out of his pocket, and proffered it silently

"That bad, hunh?" She combed her hair with no flourishes, down from the crown around her face, ears and neck. Thank God her hair—and the rest of her—was at least clean. He tried to remember where he'd seen a haircut like that on a woman before. Aha! It was an actress in a road-company production of Shaw's *Saint Joan*.

The unsaintly Juanita pointed, said "That way," slapped his comb back in his palm, and took off.

When the sun was at its Georgia summer worst, they stopped by a creek to eat the anchovies. "Long time since I used one of these goddamn' keys," he grunted, twisting the nastily-sharp little tin ribbon off the can.

"One of civilization's refinements we *don't* miss."

It occurred to him that he knew nothing about her, other than her murderous present. He started gingerly. "You know, even at this late date if they told me my home town was all in one piece, I don't know but what I'd desert and go home."

"Where's that?"

"Gastonia, North Carolina." She went "mmph" so he went on. "When it came, I was lucky enough to be taking off on patrol, out of Homestead. F-14. We heard it all on the radio. Saw the flashes. By the time our tanks were empty, I knew it was all over, in Florida, anyway. Hell, all we did was dodge the warheads and circle."

"And?" She nervously fingered the safety on the Walther.

"Rest of the wing thought they could fly back to base and refuel." They shared a sour laugh. "I just dumped my bird in the Gulf, got in my raft, and headed for a place that wasn't on fire."

He stopped, because post-war etiquette held that this was

the polite place for her to contribute *her* story. She was silent. "Well, whoever you are, where were *you?*"

"I was between Salt Lake City and Denver, in a Hertz car, because the Denver airport was snowed in." She was absentmindedly digging a hole in the red dirt to bury the telltale anchovy cans. "I had to make a meeting that night, in Denver, or my whole schedule for the week would be blown." She started laughing, almost hysterically, and clamped both hands over her mouth. Bo laughed, too. It was the first funny thing she'd ever said.

"Talk about blown schedules!"

"Well, you know it was near Christmas, and the roads were busy. People going home for the holidays, and a lot of trucks. Then I started hearing funny stuff on the radio, and losing signals. What got to me, though, was the trucks. They had CBs, and I guess they were hearing about the bombs, from truck to truck by radio. They all slowed down, almost to a crawl. And stopped. I saw a guy, in a Mayflower van out of Seattle, bent over the wheel crying his heart out. So I stopped, too."

"What did he say?"

"He said, and I remember distinctly, 'Lady, we're done for. They have sneak-attacked us again, and wiped out the U.S. of A.' I stopped at the next phone and tried to call home, but... Then I tanked the car up at a station. Nobody there. And hightailed it south, far as I could get."

"Jesus," he said. "Everybody's got *some* story. One thing I notice—the ones that are around to talk to are the ones who caught on right away. We're the survivors."

"Quick reflexes wouldn't have done you much good if you'd been in a city, or a base." Her face was frozen again.

What the hell, the worst she could do was leave him in the middle of Georgia. "You didn't answer my question."

"My name was Barbara Mallinson," she said flatly. "I was a securities analyst for Bache. My husband was Paul, he was an attorney, with his own practice. We had a boy, eight, and a girl, five. Owen and Tisha. They were all at home but me, in New York, Manhattan, on East 89th Street."

They buried the tins and trudged on in silence. What could

you say to someone whose home and family were now under fifty feet of water?

Three nights later, they had to sleep side by side in a culvert. Nature took its course, as male touched female in slumber. They became lovers.

3.

They skirted the zone around Macon, because they saw skeletons on the crumbling roads, leaning out of rusted cars, sleeping forever beside the refugee route.

"Ah. Robins Air Force Base. That's what their target was." Juanita found the reason on the greasy map.

"Macon was a good-sized town, too." Bo found himself defending the honor of the south in the dumbest ways.

"Good enough to the *really* hot." Juanita—Barbara—folded the map meticulously and headed away from the scene of mass death. They turned northwest again around Milledgeville.

"Now this town was in the book, too," she teased. "How strange that a Yankee like me should have read it..."

"I was not the literary type. But I *do* know my War Between the States. Sherman marched through Milledgeville."

Two hard day's march, fortified by a broiled raccoon Bo snared, and they would be in Tara country. They hoped. The second evening was approaching by the time he got alarmed. "If, uh, this is really a large camp, and they have patrols, how do we identify ourselves?" He had visions of being shot by his countrymen, after all this.

"Leave it to me." She was assured. "They're already watching us. Following us, I think. So we've got to be close."

"Watching?"

Her elbow slammed into his stomach, knocking the wind out of him and down on his knees. Without a sound, she was lying beside him. Now he could hear it. Something moving, making leaves crackle, twigs snap. Juanita raised her head a bit, then sprang to her feet. "We're Americans. We're looking for Tara," she said to the young boy, who was pointing a sawed-off shotgun at them.

* * *

Despite himself, Bo gaped at the vast proportions of the Tara camp. Every cluster of trees hid at least one hut. Elaborately camouflaged sheds were dotted here and there, their roofs sodded and woven with branches. He saw signs of big guns, ammo stores. Many of the troops carried full ammunition belts and bayonets.

They were walking, he supposed, toward the Command HQ. In theory, they were under guard. He guessed he could disarm the boy if he cared to. He *knew* she could.

There was a large thicket ahead, man-made, and a deceptively lazy guard in front of it. "Identify yourselves."

"Bevis, Lieutenant Colonel, United States Air Force, presently attached to the American unit in Florida."

"Donna Wallace. I'm a courier."

"The name of your C.O?" The way this guy barked questions, Bo thought, he must have been at West Point.

"Shanahan," he barked back, trying to keep up the Air Force image.

"Wait here." The guard disappeared inside the grove, and inside the building hidden in the grove. Some time later, he sauntered back. "Our Commanding Officer, that is, General Dennis, will see you in a few hours. Meanwhile," he gestured expansively, "freshen up. Eat up. Enjoy Tara."

"It's a damn Boy Scout camp here," Bo grumbled.

"Mm. But a good place to have a bath, and a big meal." She was aiming for an open fire over which, could it be? a big pig was roasting on a spit.

"What if he calls us?"

"Dennis? Fuck *him*."

They had eaten their fill, bathed, washed their clothes, and napped by the time the call came.

The General's hut was the ultimate log cabin. There were steps up to the big porch, then steps up to the front room. The General himself held court in another room. He sat behind an antique rolltop desk, with a kerosene lamp casting flattering shadows on his face.

"Two people from Shanahan's camp in Florida, Sir!" the aide said crisply.

"Lieutenant Colonel Bevis, Sir!" Bo couldn't help imitating the man.

Juanita stepped slowly into the lamplight. "You really got a good thing going here, Bob," she drawled. The General paled, got up and circled around his massive desk.

"General!" He did what they called at military academies bracing, aligning his spine with painful perfection.

"Easy, Bob, easy." She was enjoying this. The officious aide didn't know *what* to do. "Bob, the Colonel, here, and I—we have some real problems with your security system."

"What problems?"

"Problems like a two-year-old Russkie kid could cut through your lines, if the kid was smart enough to say 'Tara.' Because you're broadcasting *in the clear*—General."

Bo looked back and forth between the woman and the man in the smart, starched uniform. *He* had two stars on his collar, and as far as anyone knew, *she* had only one.

"But that's not what brings us here, Bob." The way she said "Bob" made it slander. The aide was now trying to find some way to grovel in front of this new power. "We can discuss security, later. Like the Colonel, here, told your guard, we've got a little communications problem. Uh—will you excuse us, Major?" Her eyes drove the hapless aide back to the door before he could utter a sound. He shut the solid pine door behind him with the skill and unctuousness of a British butler. The wrought-iron latchkey slipped soundlessly into its bed.

Juanita leaned a haunch on the trestle table that held mounds of neat folders. "How's it going, Bob?"

"Not bad, honey." The General was now relaxed. "You still don't trust anybody, hunh?"

"She got the traitor in *our* camp." Bo didn't realize he was butting in till he'd said it.

"I'll bet," Dennis said with heavy irony. "No doubt we've got some rat-fucks here, too. We try to do a real good check on everybody when they arrive, but all we can really go on is how well they know the place they *say* they're from. There was one gal I was all set to ship back to the Russkies. Claimed she was from Baltimore, and she'd never even heard of the Orioles. Then somebody from Beltsville grilled her for ten hours straight. My God, she could even tell you about the Christmas displays in the stores, the day the war started. You want a drink?"

"Is the chief activity at *every* camp moonshine? Christ, yes."

"Not the only activity." General Dennis was pouring from an old bottle that Bo guessed had originally held Jim Beam. "We also grow some rather fine marijuana, I'm told." He handed them each a cup from some old, mismatched sets.

"OK, here's our problem, Bob." She saw Dennis look suspiciously at Bo. "He's cleared. No problem. Hey, I got shipped out of New Hampshire last spring. Went to the Coast. Nothing doing there. Any place that isn't hot—isn't in the desert—isn't under twelve feet of snow—they've got. Tight. Not even a real underground.

"So I did a little of the old sab-o-tage to raise morale, and hauled ass for Florida. Following orders, still. I get there, I find Shanahan's camp, we get attacked and move south. Since then, zip. No couriers, no boats, nothing."

"I'm surprised. They were always talking about how Florida was a natural redoubt."

"The fucking state is cold, man, cold. The Russkies have moved fifty miles south since I got there, and they're taking radiation readings everywhere. We can't hold anything, much longer."

"You want to try radio from here?"

"Have they finally gotten comm in gear, back home?" Bo was mystified. Back home? The only thing he understood now was her urgency to get in touch with Loyalist HQ.

Dennis chuckled. "Oh-hoooo. They have gotten real cute on comm. They're using a couple of Utes, sometimes. Not a whole lot of Utes here to translate." Juanita giggled, and Dennis started to ham it up. "Then sometimes we get a Cajun on the airwaves, and we can get about thirty whole per cent of that, even with two down-home bayou boys here to translate. One broadcast, *no*body got. Waves of code queries, we heard 'em. Turned out they had a Basque sheepherder guy on staff..."

"But nobody else does," the woman finished. "Let me try my luck. If you think I can be read, shut me down and we'll go in deep code." The General held the door for her, like a perfect gentleman. Was the cowering aide *too close* outside? Bo realized the burden of suspicion Juanita carried.

Communications—aha! comm!—was a cave dug in the side of a hill. The walls were bare red dirt, covered with crumbling clay or daub. It was dank, but soundproof and secure. Their antenna, the duty officer explained, was spread around on the ground outside, like a thousand snakes. Too bad they couldn't have a real tower, but they *were* stealing gas from the Russkies to power the generator, which made everybody feel good.

The tables and chairs were makeshift and homespun. The electronic boxes and wires and lights, however, looked miraculously advanced to a man who'd spent the last eleven years in the Middle Ages. Bo soaked it in.

"Hello, Old Stone Face. Calling Old Stone Face. This is Spic Chick. Repeat, Spick Chick calling old Stone Face." She spoke slowly, enunciating with elaborate care. The radio hummed and warbled and spat.

"Stone Face to Spic Chick. Talk."

"Alternate duty station. Repeat, alternate duty station, as ordered. But I don't hear from my loved ones. Is it all over between us?"

More humming, and some distant voices. "Spic Chick, are you visiting, or at home?"

"Stone Face, I am visiting Ashley Wilkes. I couldn't write you from home."

"Spic Chick, I'll speak to Mother. TK and off."

General Dennis ordered a round-the-clock monitor on the circuit, even if it meant burning up a lot of gasoline. They went off to sleep in one of the luxurious log cabins, and he was relieved to see no raised eyebrows at the idea they shared a bed.

"Too bad," he chuckled, "I wanted to hear a Ute."

"Sometimes I think they go a little too far," she said. "As long as we keep the Russkies confused."

"Spick Chick is for Juanita, right? Why are you Juanita?" he murmured into the curve between her neck and shoulder.

"Don't I look like a Juanita?"

"No."

"That's why." It made sense, so he fell asleep. In the morning, he asked the rest of his questions. For a moment, he thought she would shut him out.

"Old Stone Face is the High Command. It's in the White Mountains of New Hampshire, and there's a rock formation that looks like an Indian's profile; it used to be on all the postcards."

"Ok, and Ashley Wilkes was the jerk Scarlett loved, but what was 'TK'?"

"It's from the old teletype, newspapers. Means 'more to come'."

More came thirty-eight hours later, routing them from bed. Tousled and squinty-eyed, they stumbled into CommOps, feeling the dampness in their noses.

"Spic Chick to Stone Face. Talk."

"Spic Chick, the family sent you a Christmas present, and cards for Easter and Mother's Day. The Post Office sent some of them back."

"Stone Face, I figured. You just can't depend on the mail, these days."

"Spic Chick, we'll send you another present, but we want you home for the family anniversary. I know it's a long trip, but Mother wants to talk."

"Stone Face, can do. Am with child, but we'll be there for the party. Off." She put down the mike, gave Bo a wicked smile, and issued orders.

"Send a radio, no matter how primitive, down to the base. It's *here*," she indicated on the big wall map, "or was. *Find* them, and get them wired in. Let them know that Colonel Bevis and I are headed north, and we're OK."

"Will do," the duty officer seemed buttoned-up. "If they want to know, when will you return to base?"

"Before the first fucking snowflake lands on us," Bo said bitterly. He did not like the north, or the winter, and never had.

IV

1.

Departure from Tara was an improvement over their Florida farewell, he thought. Now, they were given food: smoked and dried beef jerky, powdered milk, and even Russian tea bags, with a woven basket filled with peaches and almonds. As he handed them a hot water bottle filled to bursting with Tara's best moonshine, General Dennis resumed the charade.

"General," his tone was tentative and guilty, "it's been a great pleasure to see you again. I hope we at Tara have been of service."

"Why, thank you, Bob," she said smoothly, and stepped up to his car. "Far as I can tell, your leaks are low-level. Even your ass-kissing Major is clean."

"And my thanks to you, ma'am." Dennis snapped it out, and a crisp salute with it. Juanita and Bo waved, and headed east at a brisk pace. They had told everybody they would try to stick to the coastline, for speed, but as soon as they left Tara's outer scout line, they turned northwest. No traitors could tip them and, as Juanita told him "the mountains—Appalachians—are a lot easier to hide in."

They had requisitioned new shoes at Tara. He teased, "I'm surprised at your softness, woman. I thought you'd march barefoot through a nest of rattlers."

"Not unless I have to, and not in the snow."

He fell gloomily silent, and read the map.

"Soddy, Daisy, Ooltewah. Signal Mountain." The map was a hand copy, and it showed they were nearing the Cumberland range, just over the Tennessee line. They studiously avoided any towns or forts. General Dennis had apologized for the map's quality, and bitterly regretted the absence of a Xerox machine, but the hand work gave Bo a warm feeling. "Signal Mountain was another battle..." he began.

"Another one the South lost?" she gave him her new gamine grin.

He said on impulse, "Barbara?"

"No." They trudged on a bit. She relented. "See, that name is from before. It's not what, who I am now. It makes me remember and feel soft. I can't afford that. Neither can you."

Bettina, his Commanding Officer, was right. Before they left, she'd given him a talking-to. "You're the only one I dare send with her, and we'll get on all right here, or further south, if they push us again. That zombie bitch is right. They'll keep at us until we have to hide in the *real* C-zone, unless we get help. So, go.

"But remember, I called her a zombie, and with good reason." The Commander had grabbed his sleeve in an unusual feminine gesture, and hissed in his ear, "She *is* dead, and that's her strength."

"For a dead woman," he fended the old woman off, "she's kickin' around pretty good."

"Because she doesn't care! She's fearless, because in her heart she's got nothing more to lose. Only thing she's sticking around for is *revenge*. So she'll take crazy chances to kill Russkies. And I don't want you dying that way."

"You hate her?"

"I'm sorry for her. I think whoever she was before the war I would have liked. Now, she wants to die, and I want you, I *need* you back. So play it safe."

"Meaning?"

"If she's about to commit suicide on your trip, doing one of her little bloodbath tricks, save your own hide. That's an order." The old woman's gnarled hand patted his face, and he couldn't resist hugging her.

He was astounded at how easy it was to avoid Russkies. They were few and far between, and their presence announced itself.

"We thought there were millions and millions of them."

"Nah," she scoffed. "Last estimate I heard was two and a

half to three million, plus another mill' in dependents. They've got other fish to fry, and this is a lot of territory."

"You ever think," he was embarrassed to talk about it, "ever think about Vietnam?"

"You mean, uh, about guerrilla patriots? Last-ditch warfare?"

"Yeah, and how the odds in your favor don't count. I mean, there we were in that shitty little country, with all that machinery..."

"We'd have won if we'd *wanted* to," she said.

"But everybody... thought it was wrong."

She jammed her thumb into her lower teeth, glowering. "Doesn't it seem pretty fucking stupid, now? Maybe if we'd done that one *right,* while we still had the stuff..." She shrugged and dismissed the past, as always. "Who knows? Right now, all I'm worried about is what happened to the right half of that map you're carrying."

Oh, shit. When had she seen it? He had it artfully folded for concealment, because the map they had for travel did not match the map on the wall back at Tara. Inland, near the mountains, it was the familiar map he'd memorized in third grade, though the old state lines seemed a bit foolish. But east, near the coast, was a new country. Where the coast line still followed the old lines, it was marked "C" or "TNV," for "terrain not verified."

But the big shock came as the eyes traveled north to Virginia. From Norfolk up to Boston, the coastal cities were gone. And the land around them. The Delmarva peninsula was cut in half, east to west. New York's islands were wiped away, except for a little fin-tail trace of Long Island.

"We don't know this is for real," he protested.

"Maybe there's some land above water they haven't shown. But it's got to be so hot, it doesn't matter." Her tone was calm, unemotional. As if she was discussing a test-tube experiment, not her home. Bo began to appreciate his Commander's advice.

"How long do you think it'll take us to get to New Hampshire?"

"My plan is to steal a couple horses."

* * *

Horses did not find the rough terrain of Florida hospitable, once they were required to do more than race around a sandy track for money and oats. Once the veterinarians with their magic shots of antibiotics vanished, the horses succumbed to rattlers and scorpions and heartworms and other parasites. Bo had forgotten all about horses.

But they were still prancing around the higher, drier, and killer-insect-free terrain of Tennessee. Bo followed Juanita as she slunk behind a tall stand of corn, near Etowah. He couldn't figure out how she knew there would be horses, but there they were. Three of them. Two of a color even he—his experience confined to an occasional Derby bet—knew was chestnut, and one mean-looking gray creature.

"What do we do now?"

"We wait for dark, and steal them."

"Won't they make noise?"

"Horses don't give a shit who rides 'em, long as they get fed. Take my word for it." And she was right. They grabbed fistfuls of hay, and walked smoothly into the paddock, hiding the bridles stolen from the barn behind their backs.

The horses took hay like maitre-d's used to take a gold American Express Card, Bo snickered to himself. As they opened their mouths to munch, Juanita slipped the bits between their jaws. "Wave some more hay," Juanita hissed. Jesus! Wouldn't you know she would take the gray one!

Juanita closed the paddock gate meticulously behind them, "so the poor bastards won't lose their *last* horse," and they walked the horses into the woods.

"Two questions," he whispered. "One, how did you know the horses were there? Two, why *that* mean old mother?"

"One, horse piss has a unique smell, here or in Central Park. And two, *I* am a mean-looking mother."

Mounting the horses was another humiliating experience. He was chagrined that she vaulted on the gray's back without any props. He had to back his good-natured gelding against a boulder and clamber on. He knew his muscles would ache for days, too. But no matter—they were under way, and not on foot.

2.

Following the spine of the Great Smokies, staying close to the Appalachian Trail, was an easy way to avoid radiation and Russkies. It was surprising that these gentle mountains had been such a barrier to civilization and invaders. On horseback, sometimes following the old scenic route, they could make as much as 50 miles a day. But they had to take paved surfaces in small doses, for the horses' sake. They were not shod.

The Smokies became the Roanokes became the Shenandoah Mountains on the map. Thes tended their horses from memories of cowboy movies, and operated by instinct. Juanita remarked sourly that it was the first time she had ever had to worry about *hooves* in her life.

When they got to the Blue Ridge area, even their mountain shelter was a monument to the great tide of death. There were skeletons of men and women on the overgrown roads, sometimes in or beside their pickup trucks. But there was new animal life in the forest, and by now Bo shared the woman's fatalistic attitude. They pressed on, and then ran into a solid wall of C-zone signs.

"We've *got* to be fifty miles from Philly." She sounded exasperated. Was northern radiation more serious than southern, or was she just worried about the horses? They'd been circling to the northwest for a full day, trying to get around the signs.

"What's the matter, Madame? The big, bad radiation booger getting to you, here in Yankee land?" She had the grace to be embarrassed, so he continued. "We *are* fifty miles west of Philadelphia. We're also twenty miles *east* of Harrisburg."

"Shit!" She grabbed the map and scanned it glumly. "Lancaster, York, Reading, Allentown, Bethlehem. Whole fucking state probably glows in the dark." She gave him a challenging stare. "Whaddya say?"

"I say we cut right through, and worry about it when we're sixty-five."

She snorted approval and kicked her horse. What towns they saw, the never knew. There had been conventional bombing here, too, so the hellish landscape was punctuated with impact craters. They both giggled with relief as they forded the Delaware River to the placid countryside of New Jersey. From there, they picked up the pace. Their goals were the Hudson River, north and then east to the Green Mountains of Vermont. It was easy. They saw no Russkies, no forts, and no Americans (though sometimes Bo fantasized there were faces behind the trees as he rode by).

"Not surprising," Juanita said bitterly. "They blew the bejesus out of the coastline, all the way down to Virginia. A lot of the northeast *is* hot. There's no oil. No oranges. No wheat. No lumber, at least not for easy harvesting, like Oregon. I've been through here three times. Never seen one of the motherfuckers north of Virginia, 'cept for recon planes."

"But where are the Americans?"

"Around here, mostly hiding, I'd guess. But up north a bit, they're just living where they always did. That's why we . . . they located HQ here." She corrected her slip smoothly, but he got it. So the guerrilla General was a member of the High Command.

Looking east from the Green Mountains of Vermont, you couldn't believe the war had happened. They climbed gingerly down the east faces, leading his "Ashley" and her "Ghost."

There was no question but that Juanita knew this territory. She no longer asked to see the map at all. When they reached the road, she trotted her horse casually on the soft asphalt that couldn't hurt its hooves, to the town limits of Ascutney, Vermont.

The sign still stood, and the town still stood, although some of the old electricity and phone poles were down or awry. Ascutney, Vermont did not acknowledge the war.

They tied their horses to a parking meter in front of the IGA grocery store, against which an authentic Yankee in coveralls leaned with elaborate carelessness.

"Hey, there," Juanita said. All she got back was a nod. "We are looking to rest up, feed up, and head across the river. Want to see our relatives in North Woodstock." The man stopped slouching and stood upright.

"North Woodstock. Hm. No problem gettin' there." (Actually, he said "they-ah.") "Problem is, havin' a place to *stay* in North Woodstock."

"Like I said, I have friends. They used to live in Laconia. But they moved to North Woodstock, near old Stone Face, last year."

"Used to be good sickle races in Laconia," the man said. He waved them inside, and added, "Your friends just moved again." They walked through a general store almost unchanged from the nineteenth century. The only signs of the recent past were big display carrousels for Coke and L'Eggs. Both display racks now held farm produce and seeds.

Following their leader, they passed corn, peas, begonia rootings, needles and thread, and carded wool, and entered the back room of the store. It held a rolltop desk, an oak chair, a spare pine table and, when their guide opened the closet door, an elaborate radio.

"Wow." Bo admired the fancy rig, and the gasoline engine that powered it, complete with fuel tank and spark plugs.

"My name's Ernie," the man said. "It used to be a Honda." Ernie was flipping switches, connecting wires, and hand-pumping. He pulled a small black part—the alternator, Bo guessed—out of a concealed pocket in the bib of his coveralls, and slipped it into place.

The generator gurgled, belched, and pulsed. Only one of the four aluminum cylinders was needed. As the radio hummed to life, Ernie turned instinctively to the woman. "Who shall I say is callin'?"

"Juanita. Calling Mother." Ernie twiddled switches without a word, but Bo could tell her name had impressed him. The radio seemed pre-tuned to the circuit. It crackled with messages, to and from the High Command.

"Mother. Calling Mother. This is Abie's Baby."

"Abie's Baby, Mother hears."

"Mother, your gift arrived for the holidays." Abie's Baby was a long way away, and faded in and out. "The family was thrilled. And we heard from Cousin Brucie."

"Did Mother hear right?" Mother was a man with an Ivy League accent.

"Right. Cousin Brucie. He's feeling much better after that attack of flu. Your chicken soup really pulled him through."

Bo stared at Juanita, who was smiling at the pine floor. He touched her forearm.

"Did you get that?" she said. "Two shipments—arms, drugs, food, whatever—both arrived on time. We're really getting it together. Finally."

"Could we call Florida?"

She made an impatient gesture, brushing the flats of her palms over her thighs, then relented. "After HQ, if there's air time."

Ernie tried to break in. "Mothah . . ." but he was cut off by a woman with a broad black accent.

"Mothah," she drawled. "Can you heah Lurleen? Lurleen callin' Mothah."

"Yes, Lurleen."

"Mothah, this packin' and movin' around is tirin' me out. My friends don't want to help, and the new neighbors think I'm ruinin' property values." Bo saw Juanita tense. So did Ernie.

"Lurleen can I send some family to help you?"

"Well, I hates to be lazy . . ." Lurleen whined elaborately. "But I does think this job is just too big for me, 'way ah feels now."

"Lurleen, take care of yourself." There was a moment's hum, as the man who manned Mother's switchboard got orders. "Lurleen. Lurleen. Move immediately. Immediately. Do you hear Mother, Lurleen?"

"I hear you, Mother." Now the black woman's voice was crisp and decisive, and there was the sound of guns behind it. "We are pulling out. West. Send help."

Silence. Then Mother spoke again. "This is Mother, to any of the family who knows where Lurleen is. Lurleen needs your help. Repeat, needs your help. Call Mother if you make contact . . ." A voice answered. But nobody at Ernie's could understand, because it was in a strange language. Ernie waited for the first pause.

"Mother, this is Ethan Allen calling Mother."

"Talk to Mother, Ethan."

"Mother, I have a guest named Juanita." She took the microphone from Ernie's gnarled hand."

"Almost home, Mother."

"Mother looks forward to seeing you, Juanita. We have a lot to talk about. Off."

Juanita shrugged. She handed the mike back to Ernie. "What circuit do you use to talk directly to other bases?"

"All different. Depends on what their radio operator thinks is his lucky number."

"Oh, great," Bo snarled.

"You heard anything from a camp down South, in Florida, on Lake Rousseau? The Withlacoochee River?"

"The *what* river? Anyways, I thought it was all hot down there."

"*We* thought it was all hot up here."

"The Commander's name is Shanahan," Juanita continued smoothly. First name, Bettina. Ring any bells?"

"Nope."

"Shit," Bo grumped. "It got fucked up again. We sent a radio from Tara . . ."

"Tara? You want to talk to Tara?" Ernie began fiddling with his dials again. In minutes, he established that a new Florida station was calling in, with the name "Ella."

"Ella, this is Cousin Juanita calling. Come in Ella."

"This is Ella," the wavering voice said, "answering Juanita."

"Ella, this is your wandering boy Beauregard. Is Aunt Betty there?"

3.

Lying in a real bunk bed, on a real mattress, he marvelled at the changes in his life. Eleven years he had spent in the Stone Age—the Middle Ages at best. Now he was transported to a village that lived as everyone had only a century before. He was deeply tempted to just bail out of the uprising right here. He could farm the soil, milk the cows, burn the lumber—and the Russkies would never come after him, and he would never dream again of that agonized mob dying from radiation sickness.

"It's really very nice here," he murmured to the top bunk, snuggling into his goosedown pillow. A head snapped over the bunk's edge.

"Nice? It's *nice* here because it's not worth their trouble to come in and kill us. Not *yet*." The head vanished.

"Did I say something wrong?"

He intended irony, but she was not amused. "No, oh, nooo. Nothing wrong at all with just rolling over and letting them grab hold of everything else. What the hell, by the time we're old, they'll just be getting 'round to taking over this area, too. So we'll have *no* hiding place." The voice dripped acid from the upper bunk. She was right, but he couldn't bring himself to say so.

Ernie and his wife confounded both of them with a breakfast of fried eggs and bacon.

They had smelled bacon up in their room, but hadn't believed it. As Bo came in from the outhouse, he gaped at the sunny-side-ups and the red-and white strips.

"Eat up," Ernie urged. "We're not starving here."

"Bacon, wow," Bo said. "I haven't had bacon since the war." Juanita said nothing, because she was eating even faster than he was.

"Oh?" Ernie said with relish. "Then folks in your part of the country don't know the first thing about saltin' and curin' a hog." Ernie was smug, and he had a right to be. There was even a rather strange but delicious butter to go on the beaten biscuits Ernie's wife had also whipped up.

As Bo later remarked, Ernie was Johnny Carson and Bert Parks combined, compared to Mrs. Ernie. She could not be described as an outgoing person, but she sure could cook. Swooping away the last drop of egg yolk with her last bacon slice, Juanita looked pensively at the plate. "I believe . . ."

"What?"

"I believe I am about to have heartburn." She burped delicately, and signaled to Bo that they should be on their way. He was worried about leaving a gift for their hosts, but she silently placed a dog-eared paperback copy of *Silas Marner* on the breakfast table as they slipped out the door. Now where had she stolen *that*?

In his previous life, he remembered, rivers were helpful, but not important. Rivers were to swim in. To have the cows drink from. To use as navigation marks, from the air. He remembered seeing the Nile Delta from a C-140, when the American government still considered it their business to enforce peace in the Middle East.

But now the Connecticut River, the river that cleaved the state of Vermont from that of New Hampshire—now it was a river to get across.

The bridge at Ascutney was down, the natives said drily. Just their luck. The invaders had done a few conventional bombing runs in the vicinity, right at the end of the war. And the bridge was never too strong to start with. Local wisdom now held that, unless you could make an easy ford up at Windsor, you'd do best to go up to White River Junction, where the bridge still stood.

Half a day's ride and they found the town and the bridge. They were referred to the town administration, which advised waiting until nightfall to cross. "Just in case," they said.

As in Ascutney, the man in charge was the man who lounged on his front porch. He passed them on to another man, who made liquor and was the town Commander, although the title made him uneasy. "Just call me Mayor," he insisted. "It's a lot safer. And more accurate." His elaborate backyard still, a Rube Goldberg creation, gurgled confirmation. "We don't bother much with military titles hereabouts, because everybody is in the movement, one way or t'other. Ya get me?"

Juanita gave Bo the look that meant he should be the mouthpiece. "Quite right," he said. "But aren't you being a little extra-cautious, making us wait till night to cross?"

"Mebbe so. But better safe than sorry. Couple months ago, we had a big, important party pass through. Got notice for weeks in advance—they had some fellas in there were nu-cle-ar scientists, atomic stuff, had to get priority. So we let 'em stop just long enough to feed up, and sent 'em through the checkpoint right 'bout noon. They no sooner put foot on the bridge than here come twelve or fourteen jets. Russkies. Made three passes over the bridge, just strafin'. We only got four people off in one piece. Couple more are still healin' up."

"Did you find the traitor?" Juanita's voice was ice.

"We think so. One fella came all the way with them, but said he had the real bad flu, too sick to go on."

"Where is he?"

"We buried him out behind the Grange Hall."

She grinned. "Well, I'd be interested in talking to anybody about it, anyway."

Bo wanted to take a nap, but then he'd miss her Angel of Death act. Maybe, he admitted to himself, I can keep her from killing somebody, this time. So he followed her on her rounds of the sickbeds.

One woman had suffered a shattered pelvis. "I'm just hoping the damn thing will heal without an operation," she complained. She had a Chicago accent.

"Why were you coming here?"

"We wanted to help the movement, the Loyalists. My husband had been with the N.R.C., and didn't want to hide from the Russkies any more. He wanted to help."

"Where you from?"

"Wilmette, Illinois. We were up at Lac du Flambeau, in our cabin, when the war came."

"The group you were traveling with—you spot any phonies on the way?"

"I . . . couldn't tell. I was busy taking care of my son."

"Was your son on the bridge?"

"No. He died, east of Buffalo. They told me it was leukemia."

"Ah." Bo had to hand it to her. She held the bereaved woman's shoulder just firmly enough to convey real sympathy, just lightly enough to indicate that she must press on.

"Who do you think betrayed you?" she asked an old man. He had lost his right eye and his right arm hung limply from a twisted shoulder.

"If I was investigating," the old man angled his head so his left eye looked straight at her, "I'd see who it was planned this crossing and then didn't go with us."

"McManus?"

"Yeh. Him," the old man snorted. "Had one of the finest reputations in the field, too."

"Maybe," Bo broke in, "the Russkies have his family." The

old man blew a vulgar raspberry. Bo turned, but Juanita was already out the door. "Anyway, they executed him. Here."

He spent the rest of the day napping and eating. Local hospitality couldn't be faulted. There were mad promises of meatball stew and London broil if he stayed another day. He didn't see Juanita again until the sunset was making light sculptures against the White Mountains across the river.

"Beautiful," he whispered.

"Used to be a lot different. Lots of shit in the atmosphere goes to make those colors."

"Disappointed you didn't get to kill anybody?" he said bitterly.

"I'm glad the traitor is dead. Whether I do it, or somebody else does, we *need* an enforcer." Her face was calm, her voice flat and unemotional. "This is the house we stay in till we get clearance."

It was an old New England homestead, plain and sturdy. The second story was all bedrooms, and since New Englanders were conservative sexually as well as politically, he and she had been assigned bedrooms at opposite ends. But after he had settled in, she came to his room. Almost before his ears registered that the latch was being lifted, she was sliding in beside him, pressing her mouth to his.

She was a strange woman, he thought. Her muscles were hard, but the skin over them soft. The combination never failed to excite him. Impatient with the damned singlet undershirt she wore, he pulled down the shoulder strap, encompassed the firm breast with his hand, and bit the nipple.

V

1.

It was some ungodly pre-dawn hour when they got clearance. In a trance, he rode over the White River Junction Bridge to New Hampshire. His horse, Ashley, was in a trance, too.

"Fuck New Hampshire," he responded to her cheery announcement.

"Ah-ah. Remember what New Hampshire put on their license plates?"

He groped through memories of a youth spent car-watching. "Maine—Vacationland. Discover Rhode Island. New Jersey—the Garden State. New Hampshire—Scenic."

"They changed it to 'New Hampshire—Live Free or Die.'"

The bridge's faded paintwork advised them to stay to the right, Do Not Cross the Dotted Line, and that New Hampshire Welcomes the Careful Driver. Over the state line, security was much tighter. Not that there were any more roadblocks or security checks, but these were professionals. Bo spotted the military manner, and guessed some were genuine veterans.

Nobody would tell them just where they were headed, where the High Command had moved after Laconia. If there were towns en route, they were guided away from them. Each checkpoint gave directions to the next, and nothing more.

The magnificent state of New Hampshire, he brooded sullenly, was a combination of rocks and water. You climbed up a big pile of rocks studded with pines, then you climbed down the other side, worrying about your horse. At the bottom, there was a body of water, sometimes large, sometimes small. You went around the body of water, then up another pile of rocks. Bo yearned for the horizontal planes of the South.

A day and a half east from the river, the predictable checkpoint guard grilled them, and was, predictably, impressed by Juanita but not by her escort. Then he unpredictably turned them sharply north.

"If they moved from North Woodstock, they finally took our advice." The woman was smirking.

"What advice?"

"Caves! Big frigging caves, on the river, right near the Old Man of the Mountain I told you about. A bunch of us did an intensive recon of the area, must be six years ago. We recommended they put HQ in the caves *then*, but everybody bitched about being underground. Perfect hideout. Can only get there by narrow ravine. You'd have to blow away a mountain to attack 'em."

"That's where we're headed?"

"I figure. North Woodstock is on the way."

Ernie in Ascutney had offered to have their horses shod, but there hadn't been time. They still had to ride on the shoulders of the road, and the shoulders here were narrow indeed. The mountains rose up higher and higher on either side, and the river by the road ran deeper and darker. Colder, too, he guessed. Sometimes by the side of the road were overgrown tourist pulloffs, with rotting picnic tables and grills.

The guards usually hung out in these places.

They'd be invisible until you were almost past them, and they would yell "Halt!" when you were at the angle that made it hardest to turn and aim a gun. Professionals. It was a long way from Ellaville. He was beginning to worry about spending the night on a picnic table when they met, not one guard, but a squad. The squad didn't bother to yell "Halt." They just spread themselves across the narrow road.

Juanita pulled Ghost to an easy stop. "Hi, guys. How much farther to Lost River?"

"Identify yourselves."

"This is Lieutenant Colonel Bevis, U.S. Air Force. He's

number two in our Florida base, Shanahan commanding. I generally go by the name of Juanita. You can check me out with General Ferguson."

The guards looked uneasily at their Sergeant. "Something the matter?"

"General Ferguson is . . . ill."

"Sorry to hear that. He can't be consulted?" They shook their heads. "OK, then General Dornier should be able to give you a good description of me, not to mention Riley. And the head of security when I left was a bird colonel named Hanson. Rudolph Hanson."

The guard on the end walked over to the stone barbecue grill, and bent over something. They realized with a jolt that it was a field telephone.

"Wow! Been a long time . . ." He felt one of those nauseating waves of nostalgia sweep over him, and for once, she made no rebuke.

"Modern conveniences, my grandma called them." She sighed, "Modern sure is easier."

The guard clicked the handset back onto the machine, and came back to whisper in the Sergeant's ear. All the M-16s—matching guns! and uniforms!—were still trained on them, he realized. The Sergeant gave a brisk nod. "Ma'am! And Sir!" he barked. "Right up the road, about two kilometers, there's an old gas station and souvenir stand. Go to the parking lot across the road, and you'll be met."

"Thank you, Sergeant." She didn't return the salute, but Bo did. The line of men opened, and they cantered through.

Lost River was just what it claimed to be. The river vanished into the mountain, carving gigantic caves as it plowed its way down from the north. The floors of the caves were now paved with timber and divided into rooms for different functions. Vital personnel and those on duty were *in* the cave. Others lived above, in the old motel and new-built log cabins. "Mother's" giant antennae were strung up in hundreds of pine trees on and around the mountain.

An important-looking man in plain fatigues greeted them. "General!"

"A pleasure to see you again, General Dornier. This is

Lieutenant Colonel Bevis, from Florida." As they exchanged salutes, Bo realized the other man was afraid of Juanita.

"What brings you to New Hampshire?"

"What's the matter with Ferguson?"

"He's got—cancer. Of the lymph glands, I believe."

"Oh, shit." She paced around, her hands behind her back. "Well, the scientists were right. For once. How far gone is he?"

Dornier spread his right hand horizontally, splayed the fingers, and wobbled the palm.

"I'd like to see him." Obviously, Dornier would not stand in her way. She went off to another cave, and Bo was fed a sumptuous dinner. He was escorted to a room with a double bed made from pine two-by-fours, and lined with pine wood so fresh it smelled like the forest. The bathroom was down the hall. The toilets were latrines that emptied directly into the underground river. The faucets gave only ice-cold water (from *above* where the latrines emptied, he hoped). But there was a kerosene "geyser" for hot water, of the type the English had favored for a century, and soap that didn't smell like it would burn the hide off a person.

He bathed with the communal soap, and brushed his teeth with a toothbrush lying there. Communal too, he supposed. And gratefully slid between the real sheets of the Real Bed.

Why did they have sheets here in New England, when they were all gone in Florida? And, dear God, what did they use for ventilation, down here in the caves? These were both serious questions, He fell asleep.

He woke up to the noise of footsteps and talk, people bustling around outside the door. Bright light glowed through the cracks in the wall, and the transom. Juanita was wedged in beside him, smelling of the same homespun soap he'd used. The answers to the questions came to him. Ventilation? There was the transom over the door, and a hole in the wall over the bed. He could feel cold air moving on his face. The caves must have wind through them. He touched the sheet and confirmed the other answer. He remembered his mother roundly and soundly cursing the modern plague of permanent-press sheets.

"They're just like goddamn' tissue paper" she had railed at

some long-gone friend. "Twenty washings and that perma-press stuff falls apart. Now, my percale sheets—and my muslin sheets, even though they may feel rough—well, I got them for my wedding chest. I'm married thirty years, and they're still without a patch." Bo felt the top sheet again. Muslin. He tried to get up without disturbing Juanita, but it didn't work.

"What time is it?" She yawned and stretched.

"How can I tell without the sun?"

"Good point." She reached to the bedside stand, struck a match, and lit the kerosene lamp without a false move. The woman can see in the dark, he grumbled to himself.

"Surprised they don't have electric light down here." He was being unreasonably grumpy, he knew.

"They do," she said calmly. "In the command center. Water-powered turbines, from the river. But they haven't run the wiring here yet."

"I haven't seen an electric light since . . ."

"Oh yes, you have. Remember the labor camp in Georgia?" Now she was baiting him. There had been electric spotlights on the stockade wall, and the guardposts. He had tried to block it all out. "Anyway, look what I got for us." She opened her hand and revealed a brand new Squibb tooth-brush, still in its plastic case. Bright yellow, and its bristles all pristinely even. Toothbrushes were another thing he'd come to cherish, since they wore out after a few years, and there were no replacements.

"Where did . . ."

"You'll feel better if you don't know. Want to christen it?" Even in a bad mood, it was too good an offer to turn down. He spent at least twenty minutes in the bathroom, exploring crevices of his teeth where he imagined all sorts of decay on the march. He prided himself on his square, white, even teeth. One wall of the bathroom held a slightly foggy mirror. And since nobody else was there at the moment, he tried out his smile.

Still his best feature. And then came the stab of pain, just as always. Natalie was the one who'd told him about his winning smile. Dear God, how had she died? And the boys? Were they close enough to the blast area to bleed to death

66

from the million needles of a blasted glass wall? Or to expire within a few days from the vomiting and diarrhea of radiation sickness? Or did they live on for a while, to die of starvation, exposure or the lawless bands that preyed on survivors before armed Loyalist bands sprang up to maintain order. Could any of them still survive, and look for him?

He would have been embarrassed to have the woman who entered the bathroom see him cry, except that she took no notice. And he realized with a jolt that the bathroom *was* for both sexes. The toilets and showers were in stalls, but that was it. Wow! Natalie would *die*, he thought ironically. Juanita was the next woman through the door, indicating that she wanted a turn with the toothbrush. "And why don't you shave?" He decided to take *another* bath, and shave at the same time.

2.

"It's the ass end of the world down there," Juanita told the room full of uniformed men and women. "The Russkies managed to squeeze off almost all communication and traffic. The C-zones run from Mobile to Jacksonville. I guess even *they* thought it was all hot, until last year. Now they're moving south, sweeping back and forth. When I got there, the camp had hardly any idea there was any organized, rebellious force beside themselves."

"I can't believe they never got a radio," General Dornier looked skeptical.

"Believe it. In those swamps, a lot could go wrong. First radio I saw was at Tara. By the way, who let them name it *that*?" Silence in the Command Room. "It's ridiculously transparent." More silence. "Anyway, Dennis sent them a radio, and I hear they've been hooked in."

"Do you think they're ready to fight?"

"No. But they will be, on schedule. *If* they get supplies from us. Food, medicine, and guns."

"You—ah—think that some five hundred people, of all ages, sexes, and abilities—can take Valdosta, General?" The questioner was a serious, stolid man who wore two stars on each lapel.

"More than five hundred, General. And growing. Given the terrain, the lack of Russki support nearby, and some intensive training, yes. I should also mention Commander Shanahan. She's a retired WAC. Thirty-year woman. Her camp *appointed* her Commander. Had duty from Korea to Saigon. And, considering the physical conditions and isolation, I'd say her camp was better-run than Tara. You get my drift?"

"General, as you know, we would prefer to have you here, with us," the two star continued stubbornly. "But if you insist on field command—*that* field command—naturally, the decision is yours." The man spoke smoothly, his face as expressionless as Juanita's. He put his pipe back in his mouth.

"Thank you, General," she nodded briskly at him. "As those in this room know, General Riley and I have long had deep disagreements on policy, going back to the days right after the war and occupation. General Riley is—and I hope I can say this in a way that will not offend him—" a nervous titter ran around the room, "—General Riley is a builder, a planner. From the very first days, when we were scattered bands armed only with hunting guns—he has taken the long view. He stayed here at the High Command, building and planning for the future.

"I . . . followed another path. And the man who unified Riley and me—the man who united us all—is dying." There was electrified silence, and she saw that even Riley's eyes were wet.

"General James Ferguson *should* be the hero of the hour. He should be the one to make the triumphal marches, and receive the thanks of the liberated people. But we are realists here. He will be gone. I pledge to you, however, I *swear* that I will continue to work under General Ferguson's guidance, a guidance which balanced planning with action, and prudent caution with boldness. And you, General?" All eyes focused on Riley. Hypnotized, he nodded agreement. She waited one dramatic beat more. "Generals, officers—sisters and brothers. I really do not believe they can stop us now."

Bo was waiting outside the command suite, as the bigwigs filed out. They were all drained and shaken, except for his own lady. Juanita left last, looking falsely demure. "What happened?"

"Thank God for what I learned at Bache. I still know how to run a meeting," she said darkly, and clomped down the hall in hand-carved pine clogs.

He scampered after her, and shut the door of their room firmly. "Bache? This is an army!"

She waved an impatient hand. "Army-shmarmy. Politics is politics. The top guy here, Ferguson, is a goner. Riley and I, we're the two right behind him. And the whole High Command was shit-scared I'd make a big fight for the Number One spot. But I didn't," she beamed. "I told them Riley was a good organization man, and I want a field command."

"What does that mean?"

"Means as long as Riley never hears the sound of gunfire, he's a cool guy. Good planner. Methodical. Me—I want to kill the bastards. So here behind the lines is hell for me."

"Where will you be going?"

She grinned widely. "Back with you." He swept her up in a bear hug, which she did nothing to resist.

He followed her into the large bedroom which enjoyed the luxury of a rag rug on the floor. Sure enough, there was electric light in the command suite. It seemed blinding, but logic told him the bulb was no more than sixty watts.

The smell of death radiated from the bed.

The man in the bed had curly, brown-gray hair, clipped short, and he was smooth-shaven. His hair had more color than his skin did. If I were from the planet Mars, Bo mused, I would know this man was dying.

"Glad to see you're awake, General." Juanita knelt beside the bed and clasped the man's hand familiarly between her own. Like a daughter.

"When they told me you were here, I made them stop giving me dope." Ferguson's voice reeked of Boston. "What happened at the meeting?"

"I did—the right thing. Riley Commands Ops. I command in Florida."

"You still think your theory holds?"

"Now that I've been there, I'm sure. The West is out of the

question. We make the first blow in the east—*all* along the seaboard—and I think the impact will carry west. But not vice-versa."

"Goddamn New Yorker." Ferguson choked on his joke, and coughed alarmingly for minutes. "I still say, if you'd take the effort to get *interested* in Ops . . ."

"Fergy," her tone was soft, and she squeezed the bedridden man's hand like a lover, "You know me. I'm the Angel of Death! We're running a guerrilla war here, and I'm good at that. Riley's good at drawing charts, and figuring out where the ammo shipment should go."

The invalid was calmer. "You're right. You'd go crazy here in the caves."

"Even the subways drove me ape."

"And Riley would shit his pants on the line."

"We'll do it, Fergy. Swear to God."

"I believe you will." He fell back on his flattened pillow. "If this damned radiation hadn't got me . . ."

"This is for you." Out of another of her miraculous pockets, she pulled a small, roughly-carved wooden cross, oiled to golden smoothness. Ferguson grasped it eagerly, carried it to his lips with both hands, then laid it over his heart. His eyes closed, and his lips moved silently. Bo felt Juanita's fist slam into his forearm, and he pushed open the door. Outside, she began to gasp like an asthmatic.

"Oh my God, the air . . ." An officious guard raced up.

"Anything I can do, Ma'am?"

"You can get that man—" she indicated the closed door, "a priest—a Roman Catholic priest." Without further ado, she stalked off.

"She meant, ah, for General Ferguson. Are there any priests hereabouts?" Bo saw the man he was asking was as Italian as Ferguson was Irish.

"I'll take that to be an order from General Mallinson, if you don't mind, Sir. And I'll get General Ferguson a priest. You can count on it."

"Don't want to make any trouble for you."

"Naah." the guard waved trouble away. "The only one who'd notice the Old Man wants a priest is *her*." He mentioned her with such reverence, Bo was convinced she had spent years here, earning the status of a legend. Before she took up her nomadic trail of vengeance.

3.

"What did he mean about radiation getting him?" They were in the mess hall, which operated around the clock.

"He's got Hodgkin's disease, cancer of the lymph system. Odds are it's caused by exposure to low-level radiation after the war. He hung out west of Boston for a long while, right after the occupation started."

"We don't have much of that in Florida."

"Bullshit," she said. "You don't know, because nobody's there to diagnose it. Or treat it. Any of the kids in your camp ever get a real bad fever and die? Anybody you know die of liver failure? Pneumonia? Edema?"

"Now that you mention it . . ." he conjured up a parade of the dead.

"Hey, when you got no antibiotics, no fancy X-rays or chemo-therapy, no treatments of *any* kind—people with cancer kick off from the side effects. Fast. They don't live long enough so's you can figure out what's killing them." She laughed, quietly but with deep bitterness. "Another small step for mankind from the war. We don't keep them alive in agony any more. Because we can't."

"If that's true," his thoughts marched with a terrible precision, "a lot more of us will die before all the radiation is gone."

"Mm-hm. And I just hope to Christ it gets as many Russkies as it does of us." She dug into her chicken with dumplings, and he followed suit.

The food at Lost River was remarkably good and ample. But, as Juanita pointed out, they had arrived in the middle of the harvest. "Wait until February, and you'll sing a different song."

"Which reminds me . . . how much longer *are* you planning to stay?" Bo had seen the hasty New Hampshire leaves beginning to change color on his trips above ground.

"I should go to a few more briefings. Overall coordination sessions. I'd like to get a chart of all the Loyalist camps along the route south, so we can stay in touch. Say, two more days. You can be getting us uniforms, ammo, and any kinds of rations they've got."

But the day they planned to leave, General Ferguson died. The guard had been true to his word, and sent for the priest in Littleton. The priest arrived in time for the funeral, but too late for last rites. He was old and bent, and he conducted the funeral service in the dead General's bedroom. Bo saw the wooden cross Juanita had tendered was now locked firmly in the corpse's rigid hands, clasped across his chest in a supplicant's pose. The body was on a stretcher on the bed, the bedding already stripped off.

After the service, a tarpaulin was wrapped tightly around the body, which was carried out of the caves and buried at dusk. A crude, whitewashed cross was fashioned for a gravestone, and they hung General Ferguson's dogtags from it. The burial party saluted smartly, the mourners bowed their heads, and the priest signed the cross in the air, consigning James Francis Ferguson's soul to God's keeping. There was a nip in the air. Bo had heard the staff joking that Lost River, like Maine, had three seasons—winter, July, and winter. The party beat a brisk retreat back to the warmth of their quarters.

Juanita stood motionless, expressionless, watching while two men and a woman filled in the grave and patted the earth down over it. There was pain, real pain and grief on her face.

"You were—attached to him?"

"You can't imagine what that man meant to me." She didn't turn her head, or break her trance. Bo's heart sank. "Out west, right when the occupation was beginning, there were Americans fighting the Russkies. Sabotage. Ambushes. But it was like ... the way I was operating ... we were freebooters. Just pirates. Common criminals and hooligans, the Russkies said. Even when we hit them hard—and I caught them in a real beauty of an ambush, in Iowa. They broadcast that local hooligans, criminal scum were at work. I guess I believed them, too. 'Cause there was nothing else to call us.

"Then I heard about a group that called itself the United States Army. Hell, I was on the run, lost most of my group in the ambush and right after. So I kept following the rumors of the army and its Headquarters, all the way east to Massachusetts. And that man," she pointed at the grave, "made me know that I was not a common criminal. He made me know I was a patriot." Her arm dropped, but Bo's heart rose. So she *hadn't* been Ferguson's lover! He took hold of her arm, gently.

"When this is over, they *will* raise monuments to him." He felt with a jolt that he now shared her certainty of victory. It was the right thing to say. She looked up, her face astonishingly young again, and followed him.

"There's another thing I think we should talk about." What was the tactful way to phrase this? Hell, there was no tactful way. "Don't you ever worry about getting pregnant?"

"You've been worrying?" the bitch grinned. "I'm deeply touched. But you see, I was a very enlightened citizen, back before. If you stuck your finger inside my bellybutton—not that I'm encouraging such familiarity—you'd find a tiny little scar."

"I give up."

"I had my tubes tied. Not to worry, superstud." So much for that. They were headed south at dawn.

The way back was going to be better organized than the way north.

For one thing, they knew where they were headed. They had real maps, marked with American camps, code words, and supply dumps. They were given real army kits, complete with mess dishes, bandages, and water flasks.

"Goddamn!" Bo enthused. "This is traveling dee-luxe. How come you didn't have this stuff before?"

"Because they took it from me, in the stockade at Chico, California."

"No kidding? You've been in a Russkie stockade? What's it like?"

Her face froze, and she made no reply.

Their horses had been "commissioned" by the army, as the

Lost River crew phrased it. "I just commissioned four cows," somebody would say. Meaning "I stole four cows for us, let's eat."

"What the hell are we supposed to do?" Bo had bellowed. But the chubby, redheaded female sergeant snickered. "Walk till you can steal two new horses, Sir. HQ needs transport." She gave Ashley a proprietary pat, and held his bridle.

Juanita wasn't perturbed. "Glad the army still believes in individual enterprise. That's capitalism, son, don't sweat it. I'll steal us a couple of new nags before you can get blisters."

Their dawn departure surprised and touched him again. They rose silently in the cavern room, washed and packed the last of their gear. Like a good houseguest, she stripped the bedding and turned the stained mattress. They decided to eat on the road, and picked up egg salad sandwiches plus small bottles of milk—the cream floating on top—in the mess hall.

Outside the cave entrance, there was a group of officers waiting. General Riley stood at the head. "We came to wish you good luck and good hunting."

"And Godspeed," a woman's voice added. Bo gulped. They were looking at his companion as if she were an icon. An idol.

"I won't see you again until after—after our victory." Her voice was low, firm, measured. An approving murmur swept the crowd. "I said to the High Command Executive Council, and I will say to you now, that our real direction was given to us by General Ferguson. He, General Riley, and I agreed on a plan of action long ago, and it's going to work. I can do more for the movement away from command headquarters. But I will be in touch," she gave Bo a wry glance, "from sunny Florida. I hope you all have a good winter, and come next year," the murmur rose again, "COME NEXT YEAR!" she shook a menacing fist. The crowd loved it.

"God bless the United States of America!" She shouted, saluted, and slipped past the group so fast Bo had to trot to catch up with her. He saw the whole crowd behind them, beside the guardpost, cheering. They went out to the riverside road and, as usual, she did not look back.

* * *

"I'm cold," he whined, wriggling inside his clothes and an army blanket, and next to her body. She *would* have to make those extra few miles before nightfall, when they could have stayed in a nice town, in a nice house, in a nice warm bed. If they had stopped in late afternoon.

Now they were in a culvert, and he was cold. But she was already asleep. Next time she pulls this shit, he swore to himself, I'll just stay in town without her.

But the next day, she stole a brace of sturdy farm horses, plump, docile, and shod. Things looked up.

VI

1.

In the short period of time between the journey north and their return, things seemed to have progressed mightily for the United States Army. Or did he just see more now, understand more of what he saw?

They dropped in on several regional commands, all well disciplined, with radio, guards and sufficient food. He was impressed by their preparedness. "We've concentrated on the East Coast," she said. "It was the plan Ferguson agreed to, and Riley gave in. We can't supply, arm and organize the whole country, so we'll start here."

"The Spirit of '76," Bo mused. "What about the west?"

"We can't do much, before the uprising. After we consolidate here," she swatted a tree trunk in passing, "knock wood, we'll move out. But there's too much land out there, and not enough people. Not enough guns, either."

They were heading south just fast enough to escape the nip of the northern winter. Basking in golden, still autumn days, and bundling up against the chill nights, Bo felt he was in flight from the ultimate enemy. In Pennsylvania, she had boldly approached a rusted-out car, sidestepping the skeletons draped in shreds of fabric, on the shoulders of the road. The door handle wouldn't work, so she smashed in the window with the butt of her omnipresent Walther, and triumphantly pulled out a quilted comforter, red on one side, moldy blue on the other. Peering into the car, she swore. "Oh, shit!"

"What?"

"There's some Life Savers in there, too. All rotten. Jeez, I sure would like to taste some Life Savers."

His mouth watered at the memory, though he hadn't had a Life Saver since boyhood. Might just as well go around thinking about Coca Cola.

The glove compartment yielded an inoperative flashlight, and a ballpoint pen. The trunk of the car, an Oldsmobile Cutlass, held a rotten spare tire and a small tool kit, which Juanita inspected with delight.

"Don't you worry about that stuff being hot?" he asked.

"Kiddo, if this wrench is hot, *we're* hot. Might as well be hot equipped with a screwdriver, hammer, monkey wrench, chisel and, ta-da," she held them up with glee, "pliers!"

He was dreaming, dreaming about driving his Corvette down the Tamiami Trail. There were bright lights all around. Motels, hotels, supermarkets, and bars. The radio was playing loud, something by the Rolling Stones, and he was going to stop at the next McDonald's and eat one of everything they sold . . . then he was awake, wrapped in the shroud-like comforter, and Juanita had slipped out, away from him.

He had the sense not to cry out. He heard the rustle of leaves, the crackle of twigs. One of the horses neighed, in the distance. Too far away! his mind shouted, and he sprang up. He raced after the sound, over a hill. He saw the horses, ambling peacefully along. Beside them, two figures writhed on the ground.

He couldn't tell which was which.

"Get the horses," one of them rasped, and he knew she was on the bottom. Without reflection, he rustled up the horses and tied them to a tree. By the time he turned around, she was on top, and she was slitting the throat of the man under her.

Bo actually saw blood spurt in the air. Who would dream the body pumped it under so much pressure? She sprang up, looking at the corpse without emotion. "Fucker was stealing our horses."

"Who is . . . was it?"

"Who gives a shit?" She wiped the knife blade on dry leaves, and slipped it back into the leather sheath concealed in her shirt.

Dawn showed them they should be more cautious. The

dead man was a Russian, probably a deserter. He had a Red Army ID card and a YT handgun, but he was unkempt, unshaven and his uniform tattered. Juanita went through the corpse's pockets, finding a greasy comb, some keys, a packet of matches, and a box of sinister-looking cigarettes. Since neither smoked, they put the cigarettes away for future barter, ate a bleak breakfast of two-day-old rabbit, and rode on.

The Russians were operating a huge cotton plantation in northwest Georgia. "Complete with slaves," Juanita said bitterly. They hadn't seen so much wide, open, cultivated land since the war. It was planted in rows and rows of lush green plants, and scores upon scores of men and women in prison uniforms were tending the plants. Weeding, watering, fertilizing. High guardposts watched them with the eyes of Kalashnikov barrels. Sobered, Bo and Juanita slid around the plantation perimeter toward the new Tara.

Tara's guard was definitely up. They started running into patrols ten miles away. At least, so she told him. He didn't see the signs. Then they had to identify themselves, and go through direct interrogation twice.

The next guard was equipped with a field telephone, like Lost River, only this machine was of Russian make. "They're catching on down here," she said laconically. "If we don't make it any more, we gotta steal it."

This time, they met General Dennis with no charades. "Christ, I was sorry to hear about Fergy," he said. "You know we were at the Point together?"

"He mentioned that. Riley is in charge at HQ now, but we stick to the same plan."

"Glad to hear it. It's sound, just what we'd expect from a real pro like Fergy."

Bo felt a twitch of amusement, because he'd heard Ferguson admit the plan was *hers*.

"You're, uh, headed back?" Dennis' head jerked southward.

"To the boondocks. You should be happy to know there's somebody south of you to take the shit."

"And we stick to the schedule?" More and more interesting, Bo mused. So there *was* a specific timetable, and Juanita was nodding yes, it was to be adhered to.

"I'd like to use the radio for a bit, if you don't mind," she said mildly.

"But first," Dennis was fatherly-firm, "you'll eat." Bo could have kissed him.

She carried her dinner of chicken stew into signals' cave, which now sported a smooth wooden floor, a new generator, and more radios. Bo slumped in casually, and Juanita waved him in with her spoon. He sat in the back, by the earthen wall, his mind on his food. The air crackled with messages. The call names were from the cartoon strips, from Disney and Peanuts and nightmares. There were advances and retreats and requests for more supplies. "Foxfire Baby to Foxfire Daddy. Over." The voice was far, far away. "Foxfire Daddy. Over." Bo sat bolt upright. That was Air Force talk! He was opening his mouth, inhaling to speak, when her glare knocked the wind out of him.

"Foxfire Daddy, am in position."

"Foxfire Baby, hold over position. Foxfire Daddy to Foxfire Two and Three. Proceed."

The voices that answered faded, crackled, and surged on the airwaves. It was a goddamn miracle! American planes *were* flying. Somewhere.

Juanita's attention was fixed on the new radio set, with the new generator. This machine had no speaker. Whatever the operator heard through the headseat, he was pounding out on the battered, battleship-gray Remington typewriter.

"He's listening in on local Russkie circuits." Juanita whispered. "Their command is so fucked up, they report to Occupation HQ in Oklahoma *and* to Moscow, simultaneously and equally."

"What's fucked up about that?"

"It means O.C.C. H.Q. and Moscow can give conflicting orders. And they do. So the Russki Regional guy can't fart until he can get them to work out a decision. He can't make a decision, and he's paralyzed till *they* do."

"You're . . . we're going to take advantage of that?"

"Does a bear shit in the woods?" They leaned over the operator's shoulders, and read that the Commandant of the nearby cotton farm and some other agricultural commissar were locked in deadly combat over a shipment of quinine and tetanus vaccines. Each claimed the shipment was mailed to him. Whatever radio court they were pleading their cases before tried to placate both sides. Split the shipment, it urged. Failing that, it referred them to occupation HQ.

Juanita grinned and stepped over to tap the operator of one of the noisy, in-English radios. "Hi, General Dennis authorized a broadcast. When you get a chance to break in on the chatter, Juanita would like to talk to Betty's Place."

She sat back down.

"Betty's Place?" he whispered. "What happened to Ella?"

"I dunno. They changed it right after we left Lost River. I heard it in Virginia. Guess this was less specific."

He pondered. Well, yes, if you used the name Ella, any Russian who heard might figure you were one of the group they attacked in Ellaville . . .

"Juanita calling Betty's Place. Juanita calling Betty's Place." She broke in right after "Uncle Ray" finished talking to "Taki One Eighty-Three."

The voice that responded was female, familiar, and totally unintelligible.

"Oh, shit," Juanita muttered. The voice gabbled on, but its message ended clearly "three minutes."

"Yiddish! Who here speaks Yiddish?" Juanita scratched the back of her neck furiously. Bo realized he had just heard the valiant Helga Wallberg, in code.

Tara's Yiddish expert—"On a Sabbath Eve they suddenly decide to go back to code?"—was one Naomi Cohen, an Orthodox Jew and rabbi's wife/widow from Atlanta. Her wig long since lost in flight, Naomi wore a ragged red kerchief to cover her hair. Helga Wallberg was already talking as Naomi reached the radio.

Naomi and Helga held an obviously warm discussion that left their listeners baffled. They chirped "shalom" and Naomi translated. "She says it's not so bad there, apart from the food." Naomi was clearly disappointed to be the bearer of

80

good news. Tragedy was much more her line. "I told her the handsome gentleman with the dark moustache and the blonde lady who looks so brave are on their way back, like you said I should. She said good. Home is still the same, and waiting for you. Then I tell her she sounds Viennese. My parents were from Dresden..." Naomi cast a leery eye at her audience. "And we sign off," she hastily concluded, without adding that she and Helga had traded homey details from their cities of origin. Which probably drove the Cossacks crazy, trying to figure out.

2.

Tara furnished them with another luxury suite on their travels.

In the hand-hewn bed, on the lumpy mattress, Bo growled, "You thought that talk on the radio was funny?"

"You thought it wasn't? Those two Yiddishe mamas did everything but trade recipes for chicken soup. And the guy before us, Taki One Eighty-Three. How would you like to be the Russki officer that has to figure out what the hell the Amerikanski radio said today? We're going to drive them Reds right around the bend!"

He had to smile. Thinking about the wonderful, bewildering variety of American slang, Bo fell asleep.

He awoke still cheerful, and aroused. The bed was comfortable, his stomach reasonably full of real food, and there was a female body beside his, warm and limber and soft of skin. She was always tidy enough to take off her outer garments. Good start. He could smell the antique smell of homemade soap, too. It seemed somehow dainty. He snuggled closer—the shock of hair blazing on the pillow was really all he saw—and felt her shoulder. Hm. She wore a new T-shirt. Something modern, maybe even polyester.

He slid his hand down the outside curve of her back, to the waist, grabbed the bottom of the shirt, and began to work his way up, as she wriggled and murmured sleepily. When the shirt was up over her head, he went to work on basics. New underpants, too! Where had she found them?

Nonetheless, underpants on females, were to be removed. He slipped the elastic down over a silky hip, down the thighs and calves.

Now she was almost awake. "Mmph?" Delicious confusion. He slid his left hand up and under her back. Before another "mmph" could follow, he slid his body on top of hers. As always, her mouth was astounding. Like a young girl's when she kissed, almost virginal, with no lascivious movements of the tongue—except when she was paying attention to parts of him other than the mouth. The pressure in his groin was growing unbearable. What was the game between them? What was the sickness in him, that he was mad for a woman who loved to kill, and was emotionally dead?

This is *not* dead, he said fiercely to himself, grasping her flesh more tightly. Her hands were playing on his back and buttocks, their mouths were locked, and she raised her legs and hips to receive his phallus. He felt her heels touching his shoulder blades, and his very essence touching softness. Then he went crazy, and moved without thought or memory. As always.

Later, he wondered did she ever feel the same sense of abandon? Or was it an act, was she really on guard?

Breakfast was fried eggs and grits with butter. The mess officer proudly told of Tara's advances in feeding the troops.

A number of small farms operated in the area between Tara and the Russian encampment, with the Russians' knowledge. The Russians took seventy-five per cent of everything the farms produced. But now, believing in the American cause, the farmers were giving the Russians phony production figures. The remainder went to the U.S. Army in return for protection. "When Russki deserters or freebooters come around and make trouble for them, we take care of it," the Master Sergeant explained, waving a greasy spatula for emphasis.

"Deserters? A lot of Russki deserters would you say?" Juanita snapped to the alert.

"Well," the man shrugged, "maybe it's just they been here a long time. And they tell me the standard Russki tour of occupation got raised to four years, from three. And maybe it's just that Tara's bigger, so we hear more."

"You've . . . had a lot of experience with the food business, I can tell." Bo was trying to cadge another serving of eggs.

"You bet," the Sergeant beamed. "I used to be day manager for the Wendy's, right off I-75, north of Macon." He slapped another serving of grits on Bo's dish, and, since the dish was still held up so appealingly, slapped on over-aged, sunny-side down egg down with it. Thinking of the 'possum, raccoon and catfish meals that awaited at his home base, Bo scoffed it down with relish.

By the time he caught up with her, Juanita was grilling the intelligence staff about Russian desertions.

"How much of an increase—say, since last spring?"

"Roughly double. I could check my files," the Captain said, indicating old oaken cabinets, salvaged from some antiquated business.

"No, no, your estimate's fine. Why do you think so many more of them are skipping?"

The Captain rocked back in his chair, frowning with thought. The chair creaked and threatened to give way, but he didn't seem to notice. "Well, there's the fatigue factor. The occupation is nothing new any more. Not glamorous . . ."

"You mean a boy or girl from the Ukraine is no longer interested in free U.S.A. travel?" she said sarcastically.

"That's it. And there's the increasing threat of American sabotage. We can't tell from here how much more the other camps are doing, but the Russkies sure are complaining a lot about it."

"And they made their tours a year longer." Bo decided to sound intelligent.

"Yup."

"And they know you're here." Juanita spoke softly, but with deadly intent.

"Exactly!" The intelligence man's eyes lit up. "They know we're here, and they knew about the camp up in the mountains, Bluebell and the others."

Bo was trying to figure out *why* it was a good thing the Russkies knew about them, when she gave the answer. "And they're not doing anything about it."

"They can't decide *what* to do." The man seemed almost exasperated at the enemy's indecision.

"You mean," she corrected, "Moscow doesn't believe them and won't authorize action."

"That, too."

"Ever make you nervous that they mostly broadcast in the clear?"

"You mean, do I think they're setting a trap because they don't go in code?" The Captain chuckled. "Very good point. Except that in the last month or so, they've been in code even for the local stuff. They keep changing them around, but we keep cracking them. We have decoding contests, you know..."

"Contests?"

"...to see which command can break a code first. So far, some camp in West Virginia holds the record—fourteen minutes after the broadcast. They have not one but *two* math wizards from the CIA." The Captain tapped his pipe irritably against the empty tin can that served as ashtray, and began to poke more homegrown tobacco into it. "We're working on the new code they're using hereabouts, but without computers to run through the mathematical possibilities, it takes time."

"Well, they know you're here. *And* they know you're listening." The Captain grinned back at Bo and made two messy attempts to light his pipe with a burning straw.

Juanita bade a private farewell to General Dennis. The obsequious major who'd been his aide was dead—of some unnamed infection that turned into pneumonia and killed him overnight. His replacement was a lanky redhead with a cracker accent. His brains must work faster than his mouth, Bo thought. By the time the cracker finished telling Bo that Juanita would join them shortly, Juanita had joined them.

Bo had drifted around the camp newly wise in the art of "commissioning" food and other necessities. Between their official food allotment and his own acquisitions, he thought they had enough to eat heartily for five days. Tara's hospitality was better than Lost River's in one other way. They didn't steal your horses. Stung by his last experience, Bo had avoided any emotional entanglement with his new steed. Memories of Ashley were painful. Juanita had christened the new team Martin and Lewis, because Bo's horse was handsome but stupid, and her horse was a born fool.

Bo was practiced at vaulting on Martin's back without stirrups or a helpful rock, so they made a smart departure. As usual, they had a good audience. Juanita made no farewell speech. She just waved (while he saluted), shouted "God bless the United States of America" and cantered off as the crowd cheered.

When they stopped for a midday meal by a moss-lined stream that burbled an invitation to picnic, Bo showed his trophies. A small sack of dried grits, a can of Campbell's Chunky Chicken soup, and a well-cured new summer sausage as big as his foot. She smiled appreciatively, chewing on chicken salad from Tara's mess, and pulled out her showstopper—a wheel of cheese, apparently cheddar, that must have been a three-pounder.

"Cheese!" he yelped. "Where the hell can you steal cheese?"

"Vermont," she said placidly. "Figured I'd save it for an emergency. And from Georgia..." she pulled out a ragged piece of rubber sheeting, rolled and tied at each end, "guess."

He sulked.

"Smoked fish. Bass, I think. But I'd rather have Chunky Chicken soup."

He couldn't help smiling back.

3.

The guards around Tara had warned them to move fast and quiet for the next fifty miles, and they were right.

They kept running into Russki patrols, and the patrols all seemed to be heading north. Bo wondered if they were staging a raid on Tara.

"You... may be right." She pounded the ground with her fist. "Wish we could get to a radio. But I get this feeling, I pick up these vibes—that they're headed *away* from something. Not toward something."

He knew what she meant. The Russians didn't seem on the attack. They were just—moving.

"Yeah. Moving where?"

He calculated they were near Moultrie, Georgia, circling Valdosta. It was dusk and they were at the edge of the forest when she whispered, "Freeze."

One good thing about Martin and Lewis. They loved to be still, as opposed to walking forward. The two horses and two humans froze. Juanita listened to nothing for a moment, her head cocked like a dog's. He knew she had better hearing, and watched the horses' ears twitch.

She vaulted off Lewis, raised her hands in the air, and said "We are Americans. From the U.S. Army. Who are you?" There was nothing for a moment, then a figure holding a shotgun pushed through the bushes. It was a teenaged girl in denim coveralls, with ragged red hair. She was followed by an old man and an old woman.

"You been anywhere near the pox?" the girl asked.

"Pox?" Bo gaped. "*Small*pox?"

"You got it around here?" Juanita spoke brusquely.

"Plenty of it to the south. Enough time gone by that everybody's shots've worn off. Everybody that isn't living with the Russkies, that is."

"You saw it? Where?"

"Oh, I saw it all right," the old man cackled. "And I knew it when I saw it. I've lived from before the time everybody had the shots, and here I've lived till after that time. When they get big pus bumps all over 'em and they stink like the devil, that's smallpox. Half the young folks in Quitman got it. That's why we hit the road. Sara and me figure . . ."

"We seem to be immune," the woman wheezed. She clapped a gnarled hand on the girl's shoulder. "But our son and his wife, Belinda's parents here, they're gone."

"So you refugeed to protect her?" Juanita was still businesslike. "Belinda, have you ever been vaccinated?"

"When I was a baby, they say."

"She was about one and a half, or two. Then the United Nations decided smallpox didn't exist no more, and they stopped the shots."

Juanita snorted sarcastic acknowledgement. "What have you folks been doing in—Quitman?"

"Yuh. Mostly staying out of the Russkies' way."

"How do you do that?"

86

The girl sneered. "Aw, we found out if you don't have something they want, like good cotton land, or a big house, or if you're not strong enough to work the lumber mill or pick cotton—they'll leave you alone."

"That what most of the people in Quitman do? Lay low?"

"Hell, no." The old man spat on the round. "Most of the people in town, them that didn't leave—run right up to the Russkies every ay-em and kiss their ass."

Bo snickered, but she pursued.

"You say some people left your town?"

"You bet."

"Sam Akers, lives outside of town, he was a ham radio man, before the war," his wife broke in. "A while ago he started spreading stories about there still being a United States Army. Some say south, some say north of town. People been slipping away ever since."

Bo decided to get back to the alarming matter at hand. "When did this smallpox start?"

"Six..." the man looked to his granddaughter for confirmation, "maybe seven weeks ago."

"Have the Russians done anything about this epidemic?"

"Bet your ass," the man snickerd with relish. "They hightailed it north, even though they all got shots."

"And even though they got orders not to," Belinda giggled. Juanita raised her eyebrows. "They had big posters up on the barracks in every station 'round Valdosta, and officers riding around with bullhorns. They were giving them big pep talks, but the soldiers just kept heading for the hills."

"Belinda understands Russki," her grandmother said with pride.

Bo and Juanita looked at each other. So the patrols they had met were deserters, running north from the pox! Juanita eyed the trio with care. "Well, folks, it's your choice. This Lieutenant Colonel and I," she waved respectfully at Bo and the audience looked impressed—especially the girl, "...we are headed south. Your Mr. Akers was right. There is a U.S. Army camp south of here. And one north too. Either camp will do their best to get Belinda vaccinated, and you'll have a chance to live free."

Martin and Lewis were not happy about the additions to

their traveling party. Since Sara Carnes, the old lady, her granddaughter, and Juanita weighed the least, it seemed logical to have them share Lewis. But Lewis refused to move with three aboard. With two aboard, he moved, but grumpily. Martin would carry old Tom Carnes plus anybody else, but likewise balked at a trio.

Which meant somebody had to walk. Bo, Juanita, and Belinda took turns. Wrapped together in their quilt—feeling guilty at this public intimacy—the adults agreed Belinda was tough.

"Adolescents operate on nuclear power, take it from me," Juanita said grimly. "No point in feeling guilty about making *her* walk. She's probably tougher than the two of us put together. Except—mentally." She snuggled down, her nose into his shoulder. Bo realized she could have been talking about *her* kids. Owen and Tisha? Jesus, what agony for her.

And then he thought, being sure of their death is better than not knowing, thinking they might still live. Maybe that knowledge gave her strength.

Belinda was a good-natured girl, easy to like. When she started acting snappy, the third day southward, they were miffed.

"Coastline? What good is the coastline? It's gonna be all swampy and full of bugs. Nothing to eat."

All afternoon, she nodded off, propped against her grandmother on Lewis's back. Sara reached a hand over her shoulder to touch the girl's forehead and saw Juanita watching, She tried to look brave. Belinda's skin was burning with fever.

By morning, the disease was out. Belinda was randomly spotted with pustules.

"You folks go on, no hard feeling." Tom Carnes wouldn't look at Bo and Juanita.

"Nonsense," she snapped back.

"We've been vaccinated time after time," Bo said heartily. "We're safe."

"But we should keep moving." Juanita stood over the semi-conscious girl. "The Indians made sledges..." So they cut down two sapling trees, and tied them together with their emergency rope supply. They strung the precious quilt between the trunks, punching holes in it to bind it to the wood. They tied Belinda firmly in the sling, and dragged her along the way the Seminoles would have done it.

Curiously enough, the horses would move three people if only two of them were on its back. Horses were unfathomable creatures, all agreed.

They had planned to go down to the Gulf Coast, and then inch their way along the shoreline to the Suwanee. That way, they would avoid the swampy land, but run a greater risk of detection by Russki boat patrols. They followed the Aucilla River to the Gulf. The Carneses were mightily impressed by Juanita's maps, and Bo could tell they now correctly appraised his inferior role.

Nobody noticed Belinda's silence when she stopped tossing and turning. They were fighting off a malignant cloud of mosquitoes and moving as fast as possible. Suddenly, Juanita's head snapped around, and she leaped off Lewis. Walking beside the sledge, she clapped a hand on the girl's throat. She smiled. "Fever's broken." The Carneses gave glad little cries. Bo saw her lean over the river and wash the hand, scrubbing it with sand and mud.

Belinda slept all the way to Fish Creek. When she awoke, she was weak and sweaty. Bo handed over his Chunky Chicken soup as part of the get-well effort. Juanita shared her cheddar treasure, although they guessed cheese was not good for invalids. So Belinda slurped chunky chicken bits as they ate cheddar. True to legend, Belinda immediately looked better, and insisted they press on.

"You remember saying how we live in the Middle Ages?" Juanita was whispering to him, her eyes on Belinda. "Think about this. The girl's going to be pockmarked all her life." She made spotty motions over her own smooth skin.

"Shit."

"Well, at least it's not bubonic plague."

"The Black Death!" He was aghast at the thought. "Hell, we should be able to keep away from rats. Germs are something else again." They spent a glum and sodden half-hour, walking through swampy land. The horses had to be led, because they were skittish on squashy land. The Colonel and the General compiled a list of diseases they were prey to, without what they used to call twentieth century medicine. It started with malaria, and when she topped his diptheria with bilharzia, he called a stop.

"This way madness lies."

Sara butted in. "Which way *what* lies?" He could see Juanita thinking up a tactful lie.

"Look!" he yelled. "There's the water!" Sure enough, it was the juncture of the Aucilla and the Gulf of Mexico. And they hadn't seen any C-zone signs.

"Which means we've got to keep our guard up." Juanita looked gloomily at the pearly beach, bathed in the pink light of sunset.

"How's that?"

"There *were* signs around here, last time I came through. Which means the Russkies took 'em down. They may be here in force."

They turned inland, east, at the Suwannee River, having encountered only two small Russian posts, both with a ramshackle, temporary look to them.

"See?" Belinda croaked. She was leaning out of her sledge to see the signs, but wasn't strong enough to ride yet. She ate voraciously, once wolfing down an entire raccoon.

"See what?" Bo forced himself not to recoil from the hideous scabs on the girl's body.

"Those're the posters about the smallpox, the ones we had up in Georgia. Boy, I'd love to just walk in there and hit 'em with all *my* germs. Scare 'em right back to Russia."

He was appalled by the girl's grim humor, but chuckled with the others.

Where the Suwannee River crossed the highway, they turned south, to join the old Route 19. He remembered the dream he had about the Tamiani Trail the night the Russki stole their horses. Nostalgia hit him again, and his stomach ached. Reality was easier to bear.

VII

1.

The jungle was taking over the 7-11's, the motels, and drive-in movies, the shopping malls and the drive-in banks. Bo thought the McDonald's near Chiefland said it all—the golden arches torn in half by voracious vines. His gloomy thoughts were ended at the Waccasassa River, by Juanita. She pulled him aside. "We can't risk exposing the camp to..." her head jerked toward Belinda, napping in her sledge. "Go on ahead, and get the doc. Tell him when her fever started, how she's healing, you know."

"Uh—three days since her fever broke?"

"And the scabs are dry. If he can come out to look, fine. We'll meet you..." and she whipped out the weatherbeaten map. Her finger traced their route. How did she always manage to be so clean? She pointed to the northern edge of the swamp and lake that abutted on the camp. His heart gave a thump of alarm.

"What if they've moved?"

"They hadn't when we left Tara."

"When do I go?"

"Now." He reached out to squeeze her shoulder, but she pulled away, apparently annoyed at the sentiment.

As he hiked south—he didn't even bother to ask if he could take a horse, and anyway, Martin was ailing—he heard to tell the Carnes family, "Bo's going on ahead to let them know we're coming in."

Fresh from the glories of Tara and Lost River, he saw his home camp was backwards, small potatoes. Even so, it was infinitely better than the old place at Ellaville. They *were* making progress.

He'd been getting nervous as he reached the north shore of Lake Rousseau, and began to circle to the east. No sign of patrols, scouts. Nobody.

He decided stealth would be the worst approach. Like Juanita, he would walk briskly and announce himself as an American officer. Whenever he sensed a presence, that was. The preparations were wasted, because somebody in the swamp was watching him and reported ahead. They had field phones now. A party, a real squad, awaited him as he hit the next roadway.

"I am Lieutenant Colonel Bevis," he started, "attached to . . ."

"We know," said the lead man. Bo didn't recognize him, but he knew two of the men and one woman in the squad. They took him to Commander Shanahan at a brisk, breathtaking trot.

The old woman charged out onto the porch of her HQ, which still wore the sign MOTEL OFFICE—REGISTER HERE, and flung her arms around him. "I didn't really believe you'd make it . . ."

"And I didn't believe you'd be here when I got back." He hugged her. "I've got to see the Doc."

"She's not sick." Bettina clearly thought Juanita was immortal.

"Nope. We picked up a pair of old folks with their granddaughter, south of Tara," he saw the Commander nod acknowledgement, "near Moultrie."

"Don't tell me, they were on the run from smallpox. We heard there was a mass exodus. And we got vaccine, sent from West Texas."

"Yeah, good. The girl had it, anyway. She's on the mend now, but Juanita said we should have the girl checked before we bring her in, see if she's infectious."

"Well, I'll be damned." The Commander put her hands on her hips and stared at him. "She picked up a family?" Was it your idea?"

"Hers."

"Shit." Bettina scratched her short-cropped white hair. "Maybe she's turning human. Get the doctor, on the double!" she yelled at the squad's lead man. He looked like he was born with that M-16 in his hand, Bo thought. Which he probably *was*.

"Smallpox. Oh, my yes, my goodness. Smallpox," the doctor stammered. All these years, and his Indian accent had only thickened. "The scabs are now completely dry, you assure me?"

"They were dry, and flaky yesterday. Her fever was gone, and she was eating heartily, sweating a bit, but in good spirits." Bo saw that the doctor had a fresh vaccination mark on his left bicep, healing pinkly on his brown skin. "And nobody else had *any* symptoms."

Before they could send out the squad again, word came that a patrol had intercepted the rest of the party. It had withdrawn in panic and was urgently requesting orders.

"Panic? Haven't they had shots?" Bo sniffed.

"They're not afraid of the pox. They're afraid of some blonde woman," the radio operator relayed in a flat tone.

"That's uh," Bo looked at his Commander, "That's General Mallinson. Ask your patrol to escort her in."

The old woman gestured him into her private room, where he collapsed on an absurdly comfortable aluminum tubing chair with mildewed plastic webbing. She poured him a drink, in a Fred Flintstone pink plastic mug.

"Yabba-dabba-doo," he said, and swallowed.

"You see a lot?"

"Yeah. Oh, sweet Jesus, yeah. Have they told you when?"

"All they say is next year. We think they mean the Fourth of July."

Bo bolted upright. It would be so perfect! "You should see HQ," he said, fast and low. "They've got it all. Radio you wouldn't believe. Intelligence. It's a natural fortress that the Russkies can't take. An there are planes, somewhere. Did you know she was on the High Command?"

"Then what is she doing down here?"

"Her choice. Her plan. She says she talked General Ferguson into it. Before he died. It's going to be a pincer movement and a general uprising, but only in the east."

The Commander poured herself a generous drink. She didn't look too good, Bo thought. She must be pushing seventy. "The theory is, we don't have enough arms or trained people to do it all at once. Juanita—"

"General Mallinson, you mean," Bettina's voice dripped sarcasm.

"They've been calling her by that, over the air. It must be OK, now that the operation is in the works. Anyway, she chose *this* as her base."

"For the uprising."

"You were right, in a way. About her being a zombie. Her family—husband and kids—were home. In New York."

"Kids?"

"She says she only wants to kill Russkies, that's all."

"Well, let's us..." The Commander cocked an ear at the muffled noise of people outside. "Let's us try to live, OK?" They hugged again. "Tell me more."

"High Command is in the valley of the—uh, shit—I don't know the name. They call it—them—the Lost River Caverns. They've got radio antennae strung out for miles around. Lots of patrols. The equipment is—new. I mean, *really* new."

"Russian?"

"Some. But some isn't. I think somewhere they've got—we've got—research facilities." Bo spoke haltingly, ransacking his memory. "Most everybody has a uniform, and they looked regulation. Everything's organized. Quiet. Nobody knows more than they have to, that's my impression. And the whole area is totally cold, but the Russkies don't enter. Nothing they want, she says."

"I've seen New England. I'd agree," the Commander said drily.

"Or maybe the Russkies know it's too defensible? They're afraid to start a general rebellion, so they stay out?"

"Whatever," the Commander shrugged. "You mentioned aircraft."

"Yaah, I heard the calls from Tara. No question, it was a patrol squadron, on a mission."

"I'll have our guys sweep the circuits, see what they can pick up." The Commander clenched and unclenched her hands. "But I think you're right, based on what we hear."

"The radio sure makes a difference."

"No shit." She was sarcastic. "We've heard calls we *think* are from aircraft. Ours. Ships, too. Maybe subs. But all the calls come in either ghostly-like—late at night, with atmospherics, or via some relay. For all we know, they could be propaganda. Morale builders. Nothing more." Bettina took a hearty swig from her mug.

"Betty's Place, huh?" he teased. "A little cutesy?"

"All the names are cutesy. Poppa's Doggy. Nathan's Deli. There's even a station, calls itself Marilyn Monroe. Apparently the dumber the name, the harder it is to figure out."

"Good point. You think the planes and ships are phony?"

The Commander braced herself against the desk edge, and glowered at the floor. "No, so help me, I don't. Maybe it's my fatuous hopes for the future. But I believe the difficulty in picking up those signals in just good security. Why don't you ask the zombie?"

Before he could answer, there was a brisk knock on the door. "Ma'am?"

"Enter."

A ridiculously young boy entered, in uniform. "Party approaching outer perimeter, accompanied by Patrol Laura."

"Thank you, Corporal." The Commander put down her drink wearily, and picked up her rifle. "Well, Colonel, shall we greet the General?" As she passed through the door and was silhouetted, Bo thought again that she looked older, frailer than he remembered.

2.

The others had had their dinner, their physical checkups, their de-briefings, and gone to bed. Now those eerie pale eyes were boring right through her. Bettina fidgeted.

"What have you got?"

Silence was pointless, lies would be worse. "Cancer."

The zombie pursed her lips, and shook her head from side to side. "Oh, my God," she said. "Not you, too."

"Too?"

"Ferguson. And so many others. Deaths people don't even realize are from cancer."

"Well, *you* picked it up. I told the doctor to keep his mouth shut."

"Keep an epidemic of cancer secret, on top of all these other goddamned diseases? Fat chance." She snorted derisively. "Where were you right after the war?"

The Commander sighed wearily. "That's the funny part. I was down in Baja California, on vacation. Cold as the North Pole, only there was nobody to tell us to *stay* there."

"You headed north, huh?"

"Right. To San Diego, or what was left of it. I never had any primary symptoms, but some in my group did."

"Where is it?"

"The cancer? Liver. Spleen. Maybe pancreas, or all of the above. The doc isn't sure. Shit!" Bettina pounded the table, "to go this far and not see the uprising!"

"You will." The woman stared so uncannily Bettina believed she *would* live long enough.

The radio yammered that important messages for General Mallinson would be transmitted shortly. She came running, without shoes or an overshirt. Bo saw the radio operator eyeing her breasts through the undershirt, and chuckled.

"Cousin Debbie" was calling. "Cousin Debbie" was a station somewhere in the Sea Islands, off Georgia, and she/it said they would be hearing from "a new friend, Tennessee Williams."

"'Tennessee Williams'?" Bo scoffed. "Aren't we getting a little too goddamned precious? What is it, a station full of fags?"

"You said you weren't literary, and you keep proving it," Juanita snapped.

Bettina scratched her stomach. "It's—Key West?"

"Right." The women nodded at each other, and Bo remembered vaguely that the playwright lived in Key West.

"But why..." he shut up fast as the answer hit him. Anything being shipped from the Northeast would come down the coast past Cousin Debbie, and then turn west into the Gulf past Tennessee Williams.

Tennessee Williams called in three days later, and told

them he was "forwarding the good news via the Alligator." They were staring blankly at each other when the radio operator chimed in. "De Alligator in de Eberglades!"

"Welcome to the Wolfman Jack Show," Juanita grumped.

The Alligator called in the next day, violating security procedures. But then, the Alligator was so near, even nighttime atmospherics wouldn't blur the origin of his call, if the Russkies were triangulating.

"Alligator just saw a whole birthday party go past. With presents," a flat, nasal voice reported.

"Good presents?" Juanita asked the radio.

"Oh, a real sweet sixteen party if I ever saw one. Y'all are just the luckiest little girl in the whole wide world."

"Cut the crap, Alligator," she snarled. "Sweet sixteen already lost her cherry. Over and out." She slammed down the mike. "Asshole. Well, it's on its way, whatever it is."

"A new radio!" chirped the daytime relief radio op, her green eyes sparkling.

"Medicine!" prayed the doctor, who was in the radio shack treating a severe case of foot fungus with a lotion brewed from palmetto leaves.

"Guns and ammo," Bettina growled, visions of flamethrowers and Kalashnikovs dancing in her head.

The birthday party had something for everybody. The supplies appeared to have been gathered from all over, then shipped from Maine. There was food. Russian food, homespun foods from the black-market farms, Latin American food. There was medicine, most of it stolen from the Russians. Makarov pistols, the standard AK-47s, and even a few of the prized Dragunov Snipers, the rifle that was so hard to commission.

Bettina, Juanita, and Bo stood gloating over the guns and matching ammo, as they were removed from the boat. The doctor pounced on his supplies with cries of delight, and set about vaccinating everybody for everything, muttering, "This is more like it, oh, my yes."

The boat had hopscotched up the Gulf Coast, mostly under cover of darkness, and sneaked into the mouth of the river between two Russki patrols. It was so old, it had coal-fired boilers. Coal was easy to steal. The captain of the boat was a weathered old salt who immediately told everyone that he was "81 years young, and not finished yet." His flag locker stocked a variety of bogus flags of neutral nations, and his radio operators were multi-lingual.

The crew and Captain were stunned by the warmth of the weather and their reception. Back in Bangor, they reported with gusto, winter had already set in.

"Another dri—" but before Bettina could finish, the Captain had his mug in position for another drink. "I'm surprised they don't use you to deliver mail," she said lightly. The Captain's face sagged in horror, and he smote his forehead.

"Jeezus. I must being losing my mind! Hendricks!" A baby-faced crew member, who wore a machete on his belt, went running to the Captain's cabin.

There were orders for "Army Detachment Betty" (Bettina snorted) and confidential briefings for its Commander. *And* Executive Officer, she decided. She called Bo in, and they pored over the papers together.

"Sounds like you picked up the picture pretty good, Sonny."

"Yeah," he whistled softly. "Get this. 'It is vital that reconnaissance in the bombing target areas be *totally accurate* to avoid needless loss of American lives. If your strike force finds loyal American citizens within the zone of possible danger surround a designated target, they are to be evacuated immediately.'"

"Hope they do us the courtesy of notifying us just where they *do* plan to drop 'em."

"And when."

"Speaking of which . . ." Bo looked up with the Commander as Juanita approached, her pallor accentuated by campfire light. A thick packet of papers, bulging from an accordion envelope, was under one arm, and a new kind of rifle clasped under the other.

Crossing her ankles, she slid smoothly into the sitting Indian-position in front of them. "Been reading up?"

"Yup." The Commander reached behind her back on the porch, to pour a drink. As she handed it to the blonde, she glanced at Bo. Mmph. They *were* making it, no question. Bo was no actor. "What's that you're carrying?"

"Ah, this, this . . ." Juanita's eyes sparkled and she stroked the sleek barrel sensuously, "is the new American-made rifle. They shipped us a dozen. Designed for maximum accuracy of long-range fire."

"To replace the Sniper?"

"Mm." She handed it over and they examined its brutal, efficient lines. Stamped on the wooden part of the stock with a branding iron was the legend "Made in the U.S.A." Bo felt a lump in his throat.

"When?" Bettina sounded so gruff, Bo suspected her of the same reaction.

"Officially, when all the regional commands agree we're ready. Salud." She tossed back at least two ounces of moonshine. Smacking her lips, she grinned at their disappointment, and leaned forward. "Unofficially, next Fourth of July."

They slammed their mugs together in a toast, and got down to details.

"Obviously, we need a lot more guns than we've got. And field pieces. Most important is transportation, to get us *up* to and *into* Valdosta."

"Or will they bomb it?" Bo remembered the formidable security rings he'd seen around Russian encampments.

"That's up to us." Juanita shuffled through her folder. "'You will assess the strength of the occupying force in Valdosta and advise . . . blah, blah."

"You'll want to do the recon, I presume?" Bettina didn't bother to veil her sarcasm.

"I'm the best you've got." The blonde was smiling. "Face it, Commander. How many squads did you say you'd lost in Valdosta?" The barb hit home. Bettina flushed.

"You're not going alone." They both swung to face Bo. "You'll need some backup, in case."

"In . . . case. Well, OK, California should have taught me *that*." She rifled through the accordion case again. "Arms and ammo shouldn't be a problem for the assault, unless we run into something unforeseen on recon. But transport is a maybe. Bo saw, even at HQ, horses is the best we've got."

"And the damn' beasts die like flies here."

"Wouldn't it be easier to just bomb Valdosta?" he asked innocently.

"Oh, yes, much *easier*," she snarled. "And now all the radioactivity is dying down, why not heat it up again?"

"I meant *conventional* bombs." He was getting hot under the collar.

"Like we used in Vietnam? They don't do the job. And besides, we don't have enough planes. This is make or break."

The Commander broke in. "How do I go about ordering supplies?"

"Should be toward the end of the main communique..." Juanita leafed through page after page. "Aha. Page 42, graf 3. Procedures on Requisitioning."

The Commander read for a few minutes, her lips moving. "Now I *know* I am back in the U.S. Army."

"Huh?"

"Will you look at all this fucking red tape?"

"What happened in California? What did you learn?" Bo whispered, to distract himself from his longing for a cigarette. He always wanted a cigarette after making love, but whenever he *had* cigarettes, he traded them for food. She was silent. "I don't want to pry..."

"I was prowling around a big vegetable farm they run, out near Chico. Trying to figure out how many conscripts, how much they were producing. Should have had somebody to cover for me, working that close. Some diversionary action. A real slick Russki patrol caught me fifty yards from the main gate." She was talking without any emotion again, so he knew it would be bad. "I played dumb, like some local who got lost."

"That's why you don't wear a uniform?"

"Or carry luggage. I managed to heave my gun into the bushes, but they found the ammo, and I had the wrong ID. So they hauled me in for questioning." Her inflection was heavy and bitter. He held his breath. "And when they thought I couldn't tell them anything, they kept on working me over for fun." Her voice caught. He waited. "And gang-raped me."

She turned her head away. Bo wanted to cry, but instead wrapped his arms tightly around her. Minutes later, her slow deep breathing told him she slept, but he couldn't close his eyes until sunrise.

3.

Sigmund Wallberg, the timekeeper, announced with gloomy relish that Christmas was two days away. The Commander was shocked. That meant only six months to prepare.

Getting ready for the assault, she privately admitted, was easier than she would have dreamed only months ago. Myron Jackson was Drillmaster, after he cheerfully relinquished his post as Acting Exec. He had assembled a group of Army, Navy and Air Force veterans, men with "real military training, even if they're not Marines." These days, adherents to the American cause seemed to be coming out of the woodwork. Which made Bettina nervous.

"It's that way all over," Juanita soothed. "Even people who've been hiding in caves know about the Loyalist movement now. And may be even some of the ones who've hidden out *with* the Russkies are beginning to get scared."

"And maybe some of them are permanent turncoats?" Bettina asked sourly.

"Leave that to me." Bettina shivered at the thought. Sure enough, Juanita slid around the camp, talking to everyone. She checked radio reports, patrol lines, duty rosters. In the space of five days, two men and one woman disappeared from camp. Did they desert, or were they ... dispatched? And Bettina was disturbed to see Juanita taking Myron Jackson under her wing, teaching him her routines.

"A one-woman Inquisition!" Bettina fulminated. "Only now she has an apprentice."

"You need somebody like that, in a guerrilla operation. Can't be too careful," Bo parroted. "Anyway, *she* won't be here to do it, when we're touring beautiful downtown Valdosta."

Bettina painfully acknowledged again that Bo would go on the recon trip, with or without her approval. "You don't want me to go, I know." Bo was talking in his low, confidential voice that would seduce almost any female. "And you think the Angel of Death will be the death of me." Bettina jerked her head irascibly.

"But she *is* more than that. Up in New Hampshire, they think she's Joan of Arc. I couldn't put it together, till a few days ago."

"Put what together?"

"They way they idolize her. It's not intimidation. Versus the way she's been here."

"And?" Bettina felt the pain building again, just behind her belly button.

"After she left New Hampshire, she went out to California, and got caught by a Russki patrol. They beat her up and gang-raped her."

Bo obviously expected her to accept this as reason for the woman's homicidal mania. Why didn't he realize it might be the cover for a *real* double agent? She felt giddy with the possibilities, and sat down with a thump.

"Yes, yes," he cooed, patting her on the shoulder in an infuriating way. The pain in her belly was in full cry, now.

"So you see now why she's a little bit crazy. But," he straightened up and gave the old woman a hearty smile, "I'm sure she's snapping out of it."

"She'll snap out of when she's dead," Bettina growled. "And she doesn't much care how soon that is. So watch your ass in Valdosta."

"I'm glad you brought that up," he grinned. "We're leaving tomorrow at sunup."

He couldn't understand why she would be running around in the woods (jungle was more accurate) the day before they were to leave. She was gone all day, while he scrounged supplies and ammo, and only came back an hour before sunset. He knew now that it was 5:00 P.M., because Sigmund Wallberg had supplied him with a Bulova Quartz Accutron in running condition, as "equipment." Sigmund supplied no details as to the Bulova's origin, and Bo asked no questions.

Nobody knew where they were going, or even that they were leaving, except Bettina. At least, that was the official story. But camp scuttlebutt must have been in full swing, because Belinda Carnes wished Bo an impassioned good luck and pressed a specially-made fish lure into his hand. Belinda had a terrific crush on Bo, and hated Juanita. He noticed that, in the soft light, the girl's scars were already less noticeable.

Suddenly, Juanita was back, stomping around impatiently, running her hands through her hair.

"We'll be back in two shakes of a lamb's tail," he joshed Bettina. He noticed that she looked no better and no worse than when he'd returned from the North.

"God bless," Bettina said. He saw with dismay that her eyes were tearing.

". . . the United States of America." It sounded as if Juanita thought the Commander had meant to finish that way. And on this bracing note, they made their farewells. Sunup was no time for emotion.

They found the hidden rowboat easily, and as he started to row, following her signals, he remembered the Intelligence Officer and shivered. She kept pointing right, then left, waring him of roots and obstacles, though it was still murky under the trees. "Slow."

"What for?" The bump of the prow hitting land answered him. They clambered out, getting soggy in the process. There was a shed, and tethered to the shed were . . .

"Mules! You found mules!" he caroled. No more walking!

"Stood to reason," she said smugly. "Horses are delicate, but mules and donkeys aren't. So it was just a question of finding them."

"Easier to get on, too." Bo surveyed the animals' nice, low backs.

"But harder to boss."

This proved to be an understatement. They named the mules Stalin and Lenin for their rotten temperaments. Both steeds refused to move at odd and unpredictable times, then would break into a bone-jarring trot. They had to be firmly tethered to a tree to guarantee their presence in the morning, and still they tried to chew through their ropes.

But they ate anything they were fed, showed no signs of infirmity, and moved mostly forward.

VIII

1.

They saw the first solid, well-built Russian camp at Newberry. So far south, they mourned. But it seemed empty. And the pink smallpox-alert posters were all over the walls. They were thirty yards away, in a clump of sharp-edged palmetto, and she was staring at the camp gate.

"Problem?"

"Mmph. The gate's been forced open."

"So?" He couldn't understand her concern.

"So who did it?"

"Americans." The answer seemed obvious, and he rose to move forward.

She grabbed him by the ankle. "Let's wait and see." They tied the mules securely in the bush, and dozed off. They were awakened by the unfamiliar sound of an automobile engine approaching.

The car was a rusted-out Ford Country Squire station wagon, driven by Americans. And they had other Americans with them. As captives.

In the two rows of seats sat a party of six, four men and two women. They were slovenly, and heavily armed. Packed in the cargo section of the wagon were five more people. As they tumbled out, prodded by the guns of their captors, Bo counted a middle-aged man, an elderly woman, and three children—two boys and a girl.

The captives' wrists were bound, so they had a hard time getting out. The woman fell on her face, and her captors jeered and prodded her with guns and feet, as her companions looked on helplessly.

"Goddamned highwaymen," Bo raged. "Vultures!" Then

the impact of the car hit him. *Car!* "Where did they get the gas?"

"Russki supplies in the compound." She spoke flatly, her eyes dead as she watched. The thugs prodded their prisoners inside the gate. There was a high scream as one of the outlaw women swung her gun butt across the cheek of the girl. Bo gritted his teeth. As the party disappeared inside the gate, he looked to see his partner's reaction.

She was motionless, seemed hardly to breathe. He could tell from the angle of her shoulders, the way her hands lay palms-up on her folded knees, that she was in a trance. He waited, frozen as she was, until a shout and a door slam came from inside the walls. She blinked, focused on him, and wiggled her shoulders. "It's really—none of our business."

"Bullshit," he said.

"Right. We'll wait until dark."

Stalin and Lenin were stolidly devouring everything in sight. Grass. Palmetto. Shrubbery. Bark. Bo realized he'd never heard either mule make a noise, other than happy snuffling sounds when food was entering their front end or exiting their rear.

They filled their canteens in the sulfurous stream, ate some powerful beef jerky from Betty's Place, and napped some more. He leaned against a little hillock to rest, first checking to see if it had been constructed by any kind of ambitious ants.

The next thing he felt was a light slap on his ankle. He was well enough trained by now to make no sound and he sprung bolt upright. Juanita hiked a thumb in the direction of the compound, and they oozed toward it with skillful silence.

It was a crude stockade, built partly of wooden stakes, partly of steel bulkheads, partly encompassing the outer walls of the houses that made up the square. If it hadn't been for the steel parts, it could have passed for a fort in a Hollywood B western. Oh yes, the radio antennae marred the effect, too, but they were sagging and rusty from disuse. He nudged her, and pointed. "Been a while since the Russkies used *that* radio."

She glowered. "Pretty nauseating idea. It took the small-pox to drive them out. Think we should recognize the pox as an official ally?"

They circled the walls, looking for weak spots and crevices, but there were none. Back facing the gates again, he swore, "Jeeeesus Christ!"

"Huh?"

"Been so long, I forgot the damned things *move*. We use the car!"

"Ah, but why didn't they?"

He was stymied. Why didn't the outlaws take their gassed-up Country Squire inside, since it was such a priceless trea-sure?

"Because they can't, for some reason," she answered his thoughts. "Cover me."

With the usual difficulty, he tried to track her progress through the thigh-high grass. She must be part snake, he marveled. He *did* see her light head bob up to peer through the chinks in the gate, moving left to right. Then the green-ery undulated back toward his hiding place.

"The Russkies left a big fucking dump truck right inside the gate, to block it. There's about—seven feet clear. Maybe if we hit it fast enough . . ." she shrugged fatalistically.

"OK, I'll hot-wire the wagon."

"Let me get under the hood to hold the switch till she's ready to fire up." They clasped hands for a moment, more like blood brothers than lovers.

It had been years, decades, but the movements still came to him automatically from his misspent youth. When you want to use the car without your parents knowing, your first step is to open the door from the *inside*, so the door catch makes less noise. He reached a hand through the vent window, his knife already in the other hand to cut the wires.

Juanita had the hood up with no more noise than the click of a cigarette case. Cigarettes! He had pangs at the most inconvenient times. He saw her bottom sticking out from under the hood, then she was giving him the high sign.

He fumbled among the radio wires, ignition wires, speed-ometer wires, God knew what. Aha! There it was. Clip clip.

Twist, twist. He sat up and raised his hands, palms up, hopefully.

"Open the other door," she hissed. He leaned over to get the door as he had on many an uncouth teenage date. "Is it in Park?"

"Whoops!" Good point. He flipped the lever on the gearshift to "p"—thank God it was automatic transmission; he wasn't sure he could remember how to do a stick-shift. She bent over again, and there was a grinding sound, then the cylinders were pounding away. The car was straining to get loose of its gears. She slammed the hood down with a crash, and vaulted into the passenger seat.

"Go!" Like James Dean in *Rebel Without a Cause*, he gave it the gas. The Ford's rusty snout leapt forward, hit the wooden stockade gate and smashed it over. The Ford met its match in the ancient Reo truck parked just beyond, but by the time it hit, both of its front doors were open and both occupants moving fast for cover.

Bo found sanctuary in a junky heap of car parts, wooden crates with Russian markings, and various decaying items he chose not to think about. Swiveling, he saw his companion make a running dive under the porch of the house with lighted windows. Its door banged open, and a fat silhouette filled the brightly lit oblong.

"What the hell?" Other voices yelled "Get your guns!" and there was a mad scramble inside the house. The fat man stepped back out of view, and a gun barrel appeared.

From experience, the invaders maintained utter silence, complete stillness.

The fat man seemed to be the leader. He ventured out on the porch with his coterie. Gesturing and cursing, he delegated a henchman to inspect the mysterious ruins. When the underling checked over the car and gate without incident, the outlaws took courage. They went to the gate and tried to push it closed.

Juanita opened fire on their backs, and Bo followed a split second later. They killed everybody at the gate instantly, and when the fat man started firing from the house, Bo shot him, too.

Silence, after the unearthly racket of guns. Then wails and screams from somewhere in the house. In the moonlight—almost a full moon, with scudding clouds—he saw her ghost-white head slide out from under the house. She waggled her gun in the "Cover me!" signal. The screams and wails stopped abruptly, then turned into hallelujahs and prayers of thanksgiving. Juanita reappeared in the doorway, and waved the M16, "come on."

They stared, terrified, at Bo and Juanita. "Identify yourselves," he barked, and looked around.

While the ex-captives babbled out their story, Bo marveled. Hiding from the Russkies and smallpox, they were working a farm just outside of Newberry, until the highwaymen came. The highwaymen had stolen food, clothes, gasoline, radio parts . . . radio parts!

"We are from the United States Army Detachment at Dunellon," Juanita explained. He realized she cleverly gave directions just a few miles from the true, in case of treason. "Does that work?" She was pointing at the radio, still in place from its Russian installation. The captives didn't know. They had been locked up in the back room, all afternoon.

"We gotta let Betty know about all these . . . goodies," he muttered.

"Mm-hm." She turned back to the others, who were chafing the rope burns on their wrists. "What do you say we dig into all this food here, and make ourselves comfortable?"

"Where's the bathroom?" one of the boys said, and everybody laughed.

"First we close the gate."

An hour later, the Country Squire was inside the ruptured gate, propping it up. For a while, they thought they'd have to use dynamite to get the dump truck out of the way, but Bo pounded the clutch with a gun butt until it released the transmission and the truck rolled creakily into the trash heap.

The rescued family watched the operation intently—even interrupting their feast—and breathed a collective sigh of relief when the gate was secure. The highwaymen were well-known they said. They had been working the area for years, stealing from the Russkies. When the Russkies left, they turned on their compatriots.

"When did the Russkies go?"

"Uh," the man pondered, "we kind of lost track..."

"About a month," the old woman said. She looked fierce, and none the worse for her ordeal. She handed Bo and Juanita fat sandwiches of some meat product that tasted like Spam, squashed between canned pumpernickel bread that had a sour quality.

Juanita glared at the radio as she ate. She looked at Bo, who raised his shoulders hopelessly. It had taken him eight weeks of training to operate a plain and simple aircraft radio.

One of the boys had found some canned Russian halavah, and was waving it around. Bo explained about sesame seeds, and how good it tasted, and then there was an ear-splitting screech from the radio. Juanita was spinning knobs, cramming the last of her sandwich into one cheek like a squirrel. They heard garbled voices and vagrant wails from the ionosphere.

"Betty's Place. Calling Betty's Place." No answer. She twisted the dial again, and repeated. The fourth try got a squealing reply. She fine-tuned. "Betty's Place, Cousin Beauregard would like to talk to Aunt Betty. If she's still up." Bo thought with a jolt that it might be cruel to wake the old woman at this hour, especially since she was ill.

"Just a moment, please. Uh, who'm I talking to?" the radio asked gently.

"Spic Chick."

"Right. Ahh...here's Betty."

"Here's Beauregard." she slammed the mike into his hand.

"How do I explain where we are without giving it away to the Russkies?" he hissed.

"Start talking. Let me think."

"Beauregard? Is that you?" Betty's voice cracked. With emotion, or atmospherics?

"Yes, ma'am, it's me. Uh, we've found some stuff here you might find handy, and, uh, some people that were being ripped off. We took care of them."

"Gotcha," the radio said crisply. "Where?" He raised his eyes at Juanita.

"Tell her she can find it all at the five-and-ten."

"Uh, Betty, it's all at the five-and-ten," he repeated automatically.

Juanita leaned into the mike and said, "Betty—it's a 48-hour sale. Off," and turned off the switches.

Rather than betray his ignorance to all these strangers, Bo bit his lip and swore to ask no questions till he had her in bed. As he was enjoying the luxury of a shower—sulphurous water coming up under natural pressure, you would think the damned Russkies could afford a pump—he got it. The "five-and-ten" was Newberry! J. J. Newberry, five and dime stores all over the South, with a red and gold sign just like Woolworth's. And "48-hour sale" meant Betty's troops could—or had better—get there in two days.

Towelling off with a scuzzy-looking piece of terry cloth, he waltzed into the bedroom she'd commandeered. "Why only two days?" he asked with some smugness.

"Because if they take any longer to get here, they're idiots. And if we stay here any longer, *we're* idiots."

She was stripping the bed. The sheets were grimy, and she threw them out in the hall, grimacing. Before putting on clean sheets, she inspected the mattress with suspicion.

"You found clean sheets?"

"The Russkies were better than those pigs. You think that bulldozer works?" He was used to her lightning changes of subject by now, and envisioned the old Caterpillar that was sitting in the far corner of the compound.

"Probably."

"We'll bury them tomorrow."

2.

They slept late, and made slow, luxurious love. Bo found that easy living always made him passionate.

When they finally got downstairs, they were greeted by pleading, questioning looks.

"You folks OK?" Bo didn't know what to tell them.

"You afraid we'll leave you?" Juanita asked.

"Yes, ma'am," the man nodded. They knew his name was Les Davies, and he was a farmer.

"Don't start worrying until tomorrow night. Can you operate a bulldozer?"

"Oh, yes, ma'am," he twisted his strong, gnarled hands together.

The bodies lay near the gate, where they had been pulled to clear the way for the car. Flies bussed over them in a cloud, and they were bloated grotesquely.

"Shit," Juanita was almost petulant. "We should have searched them last night."

"Too . . . late . . . now." He spoke through gritted teeth, nauseated at the thought.

"Mm. OK, Les," she yelled heartily. "We'll get 'em in the shovel and you dump 'em."

She grabbed the bloated arms, and Bo grabbed the ankles of the first corpse. He vomited, and dropped the body. She waved him away, and the children came over and helped her swing the carrion into the iron scoop. The Caterpillar dumped the bodies on the scrap heap and made a small pyramid of junk and earth over them as a grave.

Bo was in the kitchen, sipping water and gagging when he let his mind rove. "They sure rot fast down here, don't they?" she chortled. He looked at her with pure hatred.

The next afternoon, the little girl came running to find them. They were in the fourth house in the compound, conducting a leisurely search of their loot. They were marveling over a Russian first-aid kit, which was short on bandages and disinfectants, but long on pre-packaged hypodermics. And condoms.

The tattoo of footsteps skipped across the porch, and the girl skidded to a stop, her eyes still pinpoints from looking in the sun. "People coming, a bunch."

"You see them?"

"Uniforms, Dad says. And guns."

They ran as quietly as possible, on their toes, back to the gate. Les and his mother-in-law, Maybelle, were glued to it, peering through the cracks.

"Some big group," the old woman whispered. "Got to be twenty, thirty of them."

"You saw uniforms?"

"Russkies," Les said flatly.

Juanita slammed a squinted eye against Les's peephole. Bo saw her shoulders relax, and she rolled around luxuriously until her back was against the gate. She waved to him.

As he found his field of focus, Bo saw the Russian uniforms, all right. Worn by a large group, all of them members of Betty's best, crack troops—Squad Seven.

"You bastards might have *told* us about them," Bo waved at the sinister, muddy-colored uniforms with the red trim.

"You hung up too fast," the Sergeant retorted.

By nightfall, the Davies family was helping to load supplies into the Ford and two light Russian trucks for the trip south. They were methodically stripping the fort of wiring, machinery, pipes, and fuel.

As usual, Juanita was itching to head out, even into the jaws of night. Bo appropriated a few treats, more necessities, and resignedly went to fetch the mules. He made the mistake of announcing his intentions, and Squad Seven took the mules, too. So it would be shank's mare to Valdosta and back.

"Alachua," she whispered over the map. She was reading it by moonlight, a feat which never failed to amaze and depress him.

Depression turned to alarm. "Alachua? That's where Ed and Doris..."

"Kelly," she supplied helpfully.

"Yeah, lived! It's *got* to be hot here!"

"You see any signs? *I* didn't."

"Maybe...maybe," he hunkered down, "they had some kind of bomb that was cleaner than we knew. Less residual radiation."

"Maybe...maybe," she mocked, "the scientists didn't know what would happen. Maybe they were just guessing. Let's check it out."

The jungle had achieved a victory greater than the Russians here. Neat little lawns with rock gardens had become fifty-foot stands of bamboo and palmetto, covering the houses they had once adorned. They slept beside a pool, because it was surrounded by clear space. Some exasperated Alachuan had solved the Florida Lawn Problem (grass of the socially acceptable variety grew here only with difficulty and cash), by cementing over the entire back yard around his pool.

The concrete was breaking up as implacable nature pushed through, and unthinkable sludge filled the pool. But it was the biggest clear space they found off the road. They circled the house cautiously, and saw all the windows blown in from the south, just as the Kellys had said.

They slunk back to the clear place, and settled in their sleeping bags—actually blankets sewn into sack shape and covered with canvas. "There's bodies in there, I know it," he shuddered.

"Long dead, Babe," she said. "Long dead and gone to heaven or hell." She was instantly asleep, while he pondered the question. Did God give you extra brownie points for being the helpless victim in a senseless war? Or for being a murderer in a righteous war of vengeance?

It didn't bear thinking about too hard, really.

He followed her into slumber.

"Christ, this looks familiar."

"No shit. You came this way, running south from Ellaville."

That was it. There was a small cluster of sharecroppers' shacks, under a tall stand of pines.

"It doesn't look different," he grinned. The sun glinted through the pine boughs on the corrugated roofs and the tip-tilted windows. "But it sure feels different, when I'm going after *them*."

They followed standard procedure anyway. Whenever they encountered signs of human habitation, no matter how old or faint, they froze. And watched. Until they could be sure it was not a trap. Even then, they moved around the perimeter of the clearing, taking no chances.

They followed the road to Mayo, and made excellent time.

"Why does it bother you to travel easy?" he teased, as they paced each other on the asphalt. Soon they'd see the shopping center where the Wallbergs had provided refuge.

"Because *other* people like to travel easy. And I mean Russkies," she said glumly. The people they saw in Mayo did not seem to be Russians, but they didn't have time to check them out.

Then they happened on the rear end of a Russian column, headed north, and narrowly missed being spotted by stragglers in a broken-down truck. They dove into the bush and froze—for forty-six minutes by his watch.

It was back to traveling by jungle, and by night. They found a clammy nook under some over-achieving shrub, curled up in uncomfortable balls, and tried to sleep away the dangerous daylight.

3.

It wasn't quite light yet, and they were making good time across the broad, rolling meadow. She veered toward a clump of trees, and took off her pack.

"What now?"

"We're someplace between Clyattville and Quitman."

"Where the Carneses come from?" He stopped. She was stripping off her clothes. Taking new clothes out of her pack. She had stopped for a bath in a spring, just after dusk, and rubbed Vaseline all over her face. Curiouser and curiouser. When she was nude, she pulled on a pair of bikini panties that were whole and new, then a wispy lace brassiere. A wraparound jersey dress followed, then her torn and muddied boots were replaced by cork-soled wedgie mules. With a few whisks of a comb, she made even her hair look better groomed, sweeping around her cheekbones, Bo gaped.

She repacked her kit bag, and signaled forward movement. I won't ask, Goddammit, he swore to himself. I won't say a lousy word.

"Maintaining a proud but sullen silence, huh?" she grinned. "OK, here's the drill. We set up a rendezvous just outside the walls, and I go in with no gun, no luggage, just after they open the gate for the day. With luck, I come out tonight. If it takes two days, wait."

"You've got the papers? ID cards?"

She nodded. "Wallberg. Guy's a born crook. Thank God he's *our* crook." Sigmund was also running the Forgery and Documents Department at Betty's Place.

Just after dawn, they could see the walls and the southern gate of Valdosta. The gate opened, and several officious Russkies assumed their positions in front of it. Traffic—on foot, horseback, and bicycle, even some cars—began to flow through the gate. The hammer and sickle flag was run up the pole.

"What if . . . it takes you three days?"

"Then I'm dead. Run for it. Don't be a hero. Get back to Betty's Place and tell them I blew it, and they've got to get another recon team up here. They've got to take this town."

He reached for her hand and she did not resist. "Vaya con Dios."

She gave an answering squeeze. "God bless." Then she pulled a flimsy, foolish-looking macramé purse out of her pack, checked her appearance in its compact, grimaced, and set out for the gates of Valdosta. As she hit the paved roadway, he saw something he'd never seen before. She was swinging her hips in an alluring, female way. He followed her progress through the binoculars he'd swiped from Newberry. She pranced up to the guards at the gate and fetchingly showed her ID.

Nothing happened for minutes. A half-hour. Then an officer came out of the guard post and looked at her papers. Then she entered Valdosta.

This is some headache, his internal narrator said inside his skull.

This is the headache I get for looking through binoculars for seven hours, after a night of no sleep, he retorted.

It occurred to him he might need glasses. His eyes might be going bad, but he would never know unless they won this war and restored the American Way of Life.

His watch balefully told him it was eighteen minutes past

five P.M. This time of year, the sun set around six, and sunset was the Russian curfew. He screwed the binoculars into his eye sockets, and stared at the checkpoint.

He could see the guards were getting ready to end their day. Now it was really twilight. He blinked, pulled away the glasses and turned.

His reflexes were getting better. She was six feet behind him, her teeth and eyes gleaming in the bluish light of dusk, her shoes in her hand. "You came out another gate."

"Safer. Take them longer to get their records sorted out. Come on."

"Now?" He was dismayed. He was also dead tired.

She said nothing, just jammed her shoes and bag into her pack, slung it on her shoulder, and took off, barefoot and at top speed.

They were almost a mile away when he heard the alarm klaxons go off inside the town. He glared. "Tell you when we're clear," she said, and picked up her pace.

Miles and hours later, on the swamp's edge, she consented to stop. "Now!" he growled. He was too tired to sleep, anyway. She began to talk about it in a monotone.

Getting in the town was easier than it looked to Bo. The Russkies always took their deliberate time perusing papers and travel permits. They were naturally suspicious, even of their compatriots. When they couldn't find any fault with her papers, they decided to consult with an officer before admitting this strange American woman, the widow Benjamin, into their town.

The Captain looked at her papers, looked her up and down, leered and let her in. He suggested they meet at the Georgia Bay Bar and Grill later, when he was off duty, since she would be in town all day.

She agreed demurely, then tore up the ID card that called her Millie Benjamin as soon as she was out of sight. Into the record booklet all Americans were required to carry at all times—on penalty of instant arrest and a compulsory tour in a labor unit—she pasted a new identity she'd hidden in her purse lining. Now she was Helen Carney.

She acted as if she were on an important errand in town. Bustling forward, she tried to see everything.

There was a big barracks area, newly built. They were using some garden apartments as housing for enlisted people, too. Probably better than anything they'd lived in back home. Officers had the better homes of Valdosta to their own.

The erstwhile Valdosta Shopping Center, on the edge of town, seemed to be the center of military activities. It was being used as a storehouse, a drilling ground, and communications center. The town's biggest radar dish spun and hummed on top of an air conditioning tower that also bore big red letters, "ars." The Russkies had taken the capital "S" and the "e" off the front, to install a catwalk up to the radar.

She caught the cold eye of a guard in a tower, his gun pointing toward her, and picked up her pace again.

Her new ID said she was the wife of a man named Carney who worked as farm overseer for the Russkies. Improvising, she asked an officious guard outside the officers' club where she could purchase drugs for her sick husband. He refused to answer in English, but his hand signals made the route clear.

She bought lunch at an open-air cafeteria that catered to Americans. All your food was ladled into compartments of a tin tray—no dishes. The best choice in the line looked to be stew. It was abominable. Chewing on the gristly meat, she reflected that Americans who collaborated didn't seem to eat any *better* than Americans who avoided the Russians . . . just more *often*. And the imitation Coca Cola was worse than the stew. She pretended to eat, and listened.

"The Major starts yelling about how on twenty-five acres, I should have twice the crop, and I've got another think coming if I think I can bamboozle a Commissar. When I start to tell him about boll weevils and fertilizer, he says I can't get better supplies if I can't grow better crops. Great logic, huh?"

"They told me *that* was the way they always treated gum disease. No wonder they've all got steel teeth."

"They were all drunk. I mean plastered. You know they're all . . ." the speaker looked around furtively for eaves-droppers, "born drunks. But Jeez, they were wrecking the place. And their MPs wouldn't do a damn thing, because an American owns it."

"The students do not want to learn English," a sad-eyed woman in an ill-fitting uniform was saying to her companion. "They think it's beneath them."

"Never seen the stockade so full." The speaker was a long, lank black man whose voice was as relaxed as his posture. "They come in claiming their post's been attacked, and the command throws them behind bars for desertion. They don't even check to see if the troops are telling the truth." He grinned conspiratorially at the beefy white man across the table.

"That's mighty...distressing to hear." The white man's voice was heavy with sarcasm.

She had moved the disgusting food around on the tray as long as she dared. She felt a revelation scurry around the back corners of her mind, just out of reach. Deliberately, she took her tray, glass and plastic fork to the counter marked "Dirty Dishes."

In the street, she stopped to watch a Russian Army truck trundle by, its open back filled with American workers. They carried shovels and picks.

The revelation sprang forward. They didn't wave! They rode by without looking at her, or anybody else. Since she had gotten to the town, no American had spoken or waved to her, ogled her, asked her who she was and where she came from. The Russkies had really gotten to the Americans in this town. They had turned them into imitation Russkies, stolid and afraid. What they didn't know, they didn't trust.

It was early afternoon, and she had more ground to cover. She idled by the train station, pretending to wait for someone, holding a bouquet of daisies she bought from a young girl with rickets.

She strolled around the other side of the train yards, now enclosed by a high fence with barbed wire on top. Whatever vehicles were stored inside, they used quantities of diesel fuel: she could smell it. Damn! There was a crack in the fence, but there was also a Russki noncom behind her. She eyed a nearby church steeple as a lookout, but the church was padlocked, and the locks were rusty.

Then somebody started up one of the diesel-gulping machines behind the fence. Tanks. The Russkies had tanks in Valdosta.

A sign that said "Budweiser" beckoned from the window of a diner. But Bud was not on hand, only some crummy ersatz beer with an oleaginous aftertaste. Again, her fellow Americans evinced no interest in her. And the sun was lower in the sky. She checked the hospitals—one for Russians, one, a former outpatient clinic, for Americans. The only part of town not walled in was the airport. There was a big Ilyushin transport, a dismantled YAK, and a big secure hangar concealing the rest of the Russian wing. The perimeter was ringed with barbed wire and warning signs.

She was cutting through a trash-filled alley, headed back to the south gate, when she heard an engine roar, a squeal of brakes. Then a fleshy thud and a scream, quickly muffled.

The Russian soldier had the black girl pinned against the wall, with one hand around her throat.

The other hand was fumbling with his fly.

Now his phallus was out, and with both hands he was forcing the girl's shoulders down, down toward it. He switched his grip higher, around her skull, squeezing to make her open her mouth. The girl's eyes bulged white with fear and pain, and she clenched her jaw.

The Russian raised his right hand to hit her, but Juanita hit the back of his neck first. He fell forward, over the girl. As she pushed him off convulsively, she looked up to see a blonde woman, forefinger to her lips.

The girl was too astonished to speak, or move. Juanita gestured down the alley. "Get lost!"

"You're American?"

"U.S. Army. Haul ass."

The black girl scrambled to her feet and galloped away. She turned at the corner, and looked back.

By that time, Juanita was slashing the Russian open from breastbone to pubis.

"You took a knife?" Bo scowled. It was grounds for automatic arrest by any Russki for an American to carry a weapon.

She pulled it out of its hiding place, in the hollowed-out

handle of her purse. It was a switchblade, and there was still blood on it.

"Why didn't you just break his neck? Isn't that your specialty?"

She stared at the ground, and he remembered *she* had been raped by Russkies. "I'm s—"

"Right," she cut him off. "Besides, I wanted to make a bit of a stink in that smug little Russki fort. Probably a mistake."

"They'll think it was one of their own. Maybe."

"No, they won't," she grinned. "I wrote 'U.S.A. Forever' on the wall. In his blood."

She removed her mufti, and got back into her usual military castoffs. Bo shivered and knew he had just acquired a new ritual nightmare. He was preparing his sleeping bag when she spoke again.

"Memorize this, so there will be two chances of getting the information back."

"Memorize what?"

"The Russian detachment at Valdosta is not at present adding to or subtracting from its striking force or support forces." She was reciting from a memorandum she'd written in her head. "Supplies entering appear adequate to maintain present levels of staffing, no more. Estimated Russian forces— nineteen hundred army, two hundred air force, approximately one hundred health workers and occupation administrators. Cannot compute resident American population inside the walls. Daytime workers and visitors allowed inside— approximately two thousand.

"Town perimeter guarded by good security net. Gun towers, searchlights, routine patrols. Best approach point: the airfield. No walls, but probable land mines and booby traps. Food and other supplies within armed perimeter only adequate for a few days, without rail or air support." She scratched her ankle. "You got that?"

It took another hour, and Bo thought he would die first, but eventually he was letter perfect, and could tell anybody all about Valdosta.

IX

1.

"Tell me, what the hell did you *do* in Valdosta?" Bettina demanded, while Bo was still saluting.

Juanita told. Bettina blanched. "Didn't it occur to you, the Americans in town will pay the price? In Russkie reprisals?"

"Collaborators. Fuck 'em." The blonde spoke flatly, with no emotion. "You want to hear about the town, or not?" She had worked up an amateur map on paper folded myriad times to fit into a pocket. As Bettina's hands took one corner of the map to hold it down, Bo was shocked to see their frailty. There even seemed to be a slight tremor. He stared at his Commander, trying to reconcile the blustery, hearty "Betty" of a few months ago with this less substantial figure. The inevitable conclusion was alarming.

"Can we take it?" Betty squinted, and looked down the bridge of her nose at the fine lines and letters.

"Yes. Morale is bad, security is loose." Juanita started to pace around the table, hands behind her back. "Paranoid, but loose. They've had a lot of problems with desertion. Town scuttlebutt is even if a Russki outpost *is* attacked, when the soldiers make it back to command base, they're treated as deserters. Don't know if that's true, but interesting."

"What are you going to do about the Americans in town, when we attack?" the Commander asked sharply. "And don't say 'fuck 'em.'"

"Give them as much warning as we can, so they can piss or get off the pot. *Then* fuck 'em."

Bettina looked exasperated. And tired. "We *must* have more medium stuff. Field pieces. Flamethrowers. Demolition charges. Grenade guns. We can't exactly use the human wave method here."

"Write a list, and I'll talk to Lost River."

"That's another problem." Bettina started to snicker, ruefully. "I'm not even sure what the hell we *have* got. Wallberg has got such tip-top security surrounding our supply depot, even *I* can't find out what the situation is."

"If I know Sigmund," Bo said, "the entire state of Florida has been stripped bare, and is in his warehouse."

When they stepped outside, the guard saluted smartly, and said "Happy New Year, folks." Bo and Juanita looked at each other uneasily.

"How can I tell you what our supplies are, just like that?" Sigmund as quartermaster was bustling, officious, smug. He carried a clipboard under one arm, and wore khaki bermuda shorts, British-style. But they were too big for his slimmed bulk, so they were sloppily cinched in with a web U. S. Army belt. Helga bustled after him with another clipboard and a worried expression.

"We could prepare an estimate . . ." she ventured timidly.

"Estimate, shmestimate!" Sigmund roared. Helga cowered. "Security is vital, and my time is short."

Lieutenant Colonel Bevis gave up and walked away. He came back with the General.

Sigmund rolled his eyes like a horse who spots a rattlesnake. "I'm asking again, Sigmund. Let me into the depot so *I* can assess our supply situation." Bo deliberately concealed his merriment.

Sigmund rolled his eyes in Juanita's direction, and rolled them back. "Now, if you like?" he forced out.

"Thank you, Major," Bo grinned sassily. He wrapped an arm around Sigmund's narrow shoulders in false bonhomie. Juanita didn't move, but Bo knew he had made his point. He, Sigmund, and Helga approached the heavily-guarded Holy of Holies, the supply center.

The center was really a sprawling complex of wooden sheds, other buildings in various stages of construction, and open areas covered only by corrugated roofing or tenting. It was surrounded by cordons of guards whose only apparent loyalty was to Sigmund Wallberg. (He had officially been named a major by the High Command, but preferred to be known simply and absolutely as The Quartermaster.) Helga was obeyed, since she was doing Sigmund's work, but the supply guards held everybody else in mistrust, if no loathing.

"Got them trained just like German shepherds, eh?" Bo said sarcastically, enragingly. By the time Sigmund remembered that German shepherds were the dogs he knew as Alsatians— dreadful death-camp dogs!—Bo was inside the gates.

"I'm not here to take anything, or stop any of your work. But we've got to know what we have, and what we need."

"And who says what we need?" Sigmund bristled.

"General Mallinson."

Sigmund shut up. A guard unlocked a huge padlock with a key that was chained to his waist—how European!—and they went into the first warehouse.

Two and a quarter hours later, Bo's mind was reeling and his eyes were dancing in his head. He knew it was exactly two and a quarter hours because Sigmund had pressed another Bulova watch on him in the first warehouse.

"Look, Sigmund, here's the deal." He finished scribbling on his messy list. "You're obviously running a black market here. A *big* black market." He paused, to let it sink in. "I personally don't give a rat's ass what you do on the side. As long, I repeat," Bo jabbed a stiff forefinger into Sigmund's breastbone, "*as long* as you get us the supplies we need. So far, you seem to be doing OK."

Sigmund eyed the Colonel warily. He thinks I'm going to ask for a piece of the action, Bo mused. "Of course, you'd probably be doing even better if you weren't spending all this time trading in food and clothes and stuff. So let's consider this—a warning."

"Of what?"

"Of—if you *don't* get me *what* I want, *when* I want—and I don't give a shit *how* you get it . . ."

"Yes?" Sigmund was almost back to sneering.

"I tell the General. Now let me out of this—this— Bloomingdale's." Bo stalked out of the depot in fine form. Sigmund almost clicked his heels as he passed.

* * *

"Look, I told you, that stuff bores me." Juanita was decoding a radio message. It had been received in phonetic Latin and, freakishly enough, she remembered every declension from three years of Caesar, Cicero, and Catullus. "Just let me know, are we in shape to attack Valdosta? And win?"

"Like Betty said, we need more medium stuff. But that bandit Wallberg's done pretty well. For himself, too."

"I figured. The girls in camp are even wearing Russki lipstick. Soon as you and Betty and Myron can put together a complete requisition, we should get it off. This is..." she stopped translating, and started counting on her fingers.

"February sixth," Bo announced after consulting his new watch. "But a lot of our supply position depends on whether we're getting air support..." he trailed off suggestively.

She stared into middle distance. "Make the list up both ways, just to be on the safe side. But, uh..."

"I heard that radio call at Tara," he grinned.

"And, son, you ain't heard nothin' yet." She waved the decoded message, and gave one of her rare, truly gleeful smiles: "Let's get the good news to Betty."

Bo frowned. "I'm worried about her." He caught the fleeting expression, before Juanita blanked it out. "What? What is it?"

"Cancer."

"Oh, my sweet Jesus."

"Isn't it a bitch?"

"See," he struggled against the lump in his throat, the tightness in his chest, "she means to me what Ferguson meant to you." He was unable to stop it—he was crying. Blubbering. He expected a stinging rebuke, but she put a hand on his shoulder.

"I know, I know. She's been trying to hide it, though, from you and everybody. You've got to help her."

"Does anybody know how long?" he hiccuped.

"I swore to her she'd live to see the uprising. God owes her that much."

2.

God owes her that much, he said bowed in prayer.

The camp had church services now, every Sunday morning. Everybody said it proved they really *were* an army, a nation again. They could take time off to worship.

The services were nondenominational. They were conducted by Kevin O'Leary, who left the Jesuits before taking the vows, and Morell Simpson, who was an ordained minister of the Afro-Baptist Church. (There was a retired rabbi in camp, too. But as he said, "I work Saturdays.") The words to the hymns and responses were written on a big blackboard at the head of the mess tent, which served as Church, Sunday school, and regular school.

"Oh God, our Help in ages past/Our Help for years to come," the assembly sang lustily, accompanied by a battered Aeolian spinet. "Our Shelter from the stormy blast/And Our Eternal Home."

The Rev. Simpson had first suggested "A Mighty Fortress Is Our God" for the opening hymn, but realized his error when O'Leary gave him a full counter-reformation glare. Even now, after the Götterdammerung, Martin Luther and his song were anathema to the Catholics, the reverend chuckled. But only inwardly. "Let us pray," he said solemnly, and counted the house as he bowed his head.

"Our Father, Who art in Heaven..." almost everybody in camp was there. Remarkable. Before the war, if you drew ten per cent of the townspeople of your denomination, your church was a big success. The bishop wrote you glowing letters. In their adversity, oh Lord, Thy people turn unto Thee.

The Catholics fell silent, as the Protestants finished up with "for Thine is the Kingdom, and the Power, and the Glory, for ever and ever."

"Amen." As Kevin O'Leary read the scripture Morell Simpson saw with surprise that the Commander had joined them, and the legendary General Mallinson. They call her the Angel of Death, he thought, but she doesn't look so terrible. Well,

God has a purpose, even for avenging angels. They had Holy Communion with bits of soggy, camp-baked bread, and sips of stolen wine. The Catholics, after considerable consternation, had agreed to take communion from Rev. Simpson, because O'Leary was not a priest. They even took it in their chairs, like Protestants, wafers and wine alike.

The Commander looked baffled. This wasn't the way she had taken communion back at St. Aloysius in Kansas, forty years ago. The others showed her the routine, chewed the wafer and swallowed the wine. She crossed herself and thought furiously.

Bo had barged into her cabin this morning, firm and unswaying of purpose.

"What brings you out so early on a..."

"Sunday morning," he sniffed. "Time for church."

"Bah."

"Bah, bullshit. Almost everybody else goes except Wallberg. And he's got an excuse. You're setting a bad example. The Commander, United States Forces, et cetera. In God We Trust."

"You're afraid I'll die without making an Act of Contrition." He looked stricken. Men were so bad at lying, it was a wonder the world ever got in such crummy shape. Bettina took pity. "She told you?"

"I guessed. Then she told me. C'mon—they're saving seats for us up front."

"I'll go if *she'll* go," she said cunningly.

"She's holding the seats!" And he towed her off so fast Bettina hardly had her tunic buttoned before she was hustled into the presence of the Lord.

Who'd a' thunk it? she marveled. The zombie looked as though she really was listening to the service. Bettina opened her right eye a crack. The woman had the rather casual air of the Protestant, but she was undoubtedly praying or pretending to. Well, maybe I was wrong, the Commander grumbled to herself. Maybe she isn't a bloodthirsty traitor. Maybe she's a bloodthirsty killer for Christ.

"May the peace of God, which passeth all understanding..." The black minister gave the Benediction, and the congregation broke up slowly, almost reluctantly.

Many came to wring the Commander's hand, or the Exec's and introduce themselves. They volunteered for any service, even some she didn't know the camp had. She realized her army had grown beyond her, too big.

Or was it just that she was old, tired, and mortally ill?

Bo went out to use the latrine. Betty and Juanita were eating the last of the chicken off the bones. Chickens were fast growers, and their flocks inextinguishable. The camp had large pens of chickens.

"Bo told me about the cross." Juanita eyed her warily. "The one you gave the General—Ferguson? And getting him the priest. I find your . . ." Bettina dropped her tone sarcastically, ". . . piety . . . somewhat surprising."

The blonde grinned evilly over a drumstick. "Saint Paul's Epistle to the Romans. 'Vengeance is Mine. I will repay, saith the Lord.'" Bettina shuddered.

Myron Jackson was Drillmaster. He was in charge of arms training, obstacle courses, unarmed combat, weapons maintenance, and "every damn' thing you need to know to kill the enemy, survive, and win!" he howled, in the best Marine Corps tradition. Bo asked him if he didn't think that line was overdoing it. "Hell, no," Myron snarled. "*I* ate it up on Parris Island, and they're eating it up *here*."

Myron knew jungles. He knew bugs and fungi and rotten, murderous reptiles. He knew jungle warfare, but, as he said, "from the losing side." Myron remembered Vietnam. He remembered everything the Cong had ever done to run around him, get ahead of him, make him look like an asshole. He remembered, he re-created. And he invented a few new twists on the art of guerrilla fighting against a superior force.

Juanita thought Myron was terrific, and the feeling was mutual. They would howl with glee over a technique for poisoning the enemy's water supply. Tripping him with hidden wires. Blowing him to Kingdom come with snares.

"It would be nice if we could put them all around town," Juanita mused.

"What?" Bo hunkered down over a hand copy of the

127

Valdosta town plan. Juanita and Myron were gloating over it.

"Pungi pits," Myron hummed.

"Pungi pits?" Bo howled. He had heard about pungi pits from the Viet vets—concealed pits filled with sharpened wooden stakes to impale the unwary. And, the *coup de grace*, each stake smeared with human feces, to guarantee infection of the wounds.

"Hey, we're just going over the possibilities," Juanita soothed. "That's our job."

"Suppose we run short of mines? Or grenades?" Myron looked at him with what Bo suspected was false innocence. The Marine bastard would dig pungi pits for *fun*. But Bo was now carrying his notebook around, and he flipped through the three sets of entries. Category I detailed the supplies needed to attack *with* air support. Category II was no air support. Category III, constantly revised, was the present supply situation.

"Ahh . . . looks like we'll have five grenades per man in the first wave . . ." his finger ran down the smudged columns. "Mines—not many. Anyway, what do we need mines for?"

"To set up our *own* defense perimeters," Myron snapped. "Once we've taken the town."

Bo was still absorbing that, realizing he needed a Category IV, when the Marine asked, "You got any pull with Wallberg?"

"Yeah. I threaten him," Bo drawled, and hiked a thumb at Juanita "with her."

"Sonovabitch is scared of you, and not me?" Myron's honor was deeply affronted knowing that a woman had instilled fear where he had not. Then he decided to be practical.

The next morning, clad in crisp field fatigues (he had arrived in camp with a satchelful) Myron accompanied the General to Sigmund's lair.

Sure enough, the Quartermaster now understood the crying need for the little guerrilla trinkets Myron wanted. Once again, Juanita said nothing, but the message got through. Within days, a Camp cottage industry of garrote making, tripwire-and fuse-stringing sprang to life.

When dealing with non-combatants, Sigmund had a very effective approach that virtually guaranteed cooperation.

He would stand in the door of your tent, your hut, your cabin, and bellow, "You don't have to feel guilty about not being an American soldier!" Which, of course, insured instant guilt feelings, and community pressure. Then Sigmund would tell you about your vital part in the war effort, explain how simple "these little things" were to make and issue you a weekly quota.

The next thing you knew, you were whipping out garrotes or tripwires at an accelerating pace, counting the hours, terrified of what Sigmund would say if you didn't meet the quota. When the neighbors came by, you said proudly "Got my assignment!"

And when Sigmund came by and picked up one full week's quota, finished and polished, he praised you to the skies—gave you a treat of food, or drink, or clothing—and upped your quota for the next week. This technique was applied to everyone who was old enough to have learned eye-hand coordination and young enough to have their cataracts or palsy under control.

By March, even gloomy Myron admitted they might be ready for The Day.

The Commander was shriveling, shrinking, wasting before their eyes. Her head, neck and limbs got thinner, her abdomen thicker, and she had a yellowish look of death. Her skin itched abominably, and she spent much of the time drunk, to ease the pain.

Then overnight she went from wrinkled to plump and glossy skin. Her ankles and wrists grew, her face filled in a travesty of good health. She flushed, and felt her heart laboring.

"Doctor," the Exec said to the flustered Indian, "*do* something."

"Doctor," Juanita spoke slowly, "this is a case of cancer of the liver, is it not?"

"I believe so. Yes, I do, now," he nodded enthusiastically. Someone else had said the dreadful word, sparing him the agony. Because, of course, everyone knew that even when you had the very best medicine and most modern hospital, there never had been a cure for liver cancer. Oh no, not at all. You could not cut it, for the liver would not heal itself, and the patient would die instantly. The doctor nodded as he re-ran the story in his mind.

"I seem to recall, to extend the patient's life—strong diuretics?" Juanita's voice was soft and soothing.

"Yes, yes. However, we now have a policy, as you must know, General," he ducked his sleek head respectfully. "We should not expend our limited drug supply—so precious—for those whom . . ." he trailed off, without finishing. The Executive Officer looked stricken.

"You're quite right, Major." That was his rank, and how reassuring that she should use it now. "In the Commander's case, however, we might, we *should* make an exception."

The doctor looked up, seeking absolution, confirmation, authorization. "Ah. Yes, ma'am."

The pills, wrapped in a twist of waxed paper, were suggestively open-water blue. Bo and Juanita coaxed the puffy figure on the bed to swallow, with a sip of wine. They eased her back on the pillow, and listened to her labored breathing while they played chess.

"Ohh," moaned Bettina. "I gotta pee." Juanita waved Bo out, and slipped a pan under the Commander.

He was sleeping on the porch, his back jammed against the wall. It seemed there were disturbances during the night. A creak woke him, and he looked up to see the open door. Juanita stood with a groggy expression, facing the dawn. A figure came up behind her and began to complain.

It was Bettina, who had passed eleven pounds of water during the night. And was feeling fine.

3.

In early March, Betty's place was chatting with Tara when the call was interrupted. The signal vanished, and could not be raised. Cousin Debbie and Latin Quarter agreed with the camp radio operator that even the Russkies had finally figured out where Tara would be.

Days later, Betty's Place got a weak and wavering signal from the familiar voice now using the cover name of White Trash. The new station made guarded references to enemy attack, and flight. In code, General Dennis told General Mallinson that he had regrouped in the Talladega area, with diminished forces, and could not be counted on for support in the uprising.

Juanita heard the message impassively. "Nice guy," she said, "but a lightweight."

Then Cousin Debbie and Tennessee Williams began forwarding messages that a "hot load" was on its way to Betty.

"Hot load?" Sigmund snarled. "What am I, supposed to *guess* what they're sending me?"

"Us, Sigmund. Us."

As usual, the crucial call came at night, when atmospherics made long-distance calls easier to make and harder to trace. "General! General!" a muffled voice urged outside their cabin. Tender knuckles rapped delicately.

"Yo." She sat bolt upright, and sprang for the door. It was a young boy, who was night courier on duty.

"General, Radio keeps getting a call for 'Five Star Blondie.' We were wondering..."

She slapped the boy on the shoulder, and beat him across the porch. Through the door, Bo saw she was ahead of the courier as they crossed the drill ground. In her undershirt and boxer shorts (women's underwear wore out faster) she looked like a boy, too.

He heard a water-slop sound, and opened his eyes. She was sitting on a chair, candle-lit, noisily washing her feet. Which meant she wanted to tell him.

"Five Star Blondie?" he raised himself on one elbow.

"Riley's got five, now, too." She waved her feet in the air to dry. "Guess what's coming?"

"I give up."

"Radar."

"No shit?" he sat up. "Then they—we—*must* have planes!"

"Guess how they're delivering it?"

"By *air*?"

She nodded. "The other stuff comes the usual route, but

this gets special delivery. We get a call on take-off, and a circuit to radio them. Can you think of any ethnic group we haven't used for code?"

After a minute's thought, he came up with "Californians."

"Hey, bitchin' man. Boss. Super. Surf's up, and I got to go disco." She plunked herself down beside him, and he wrapped his arms around her with the thought of making love. But they were both asleep before they could do anything about it.

The did it in the morning, instead.

The American Loyalists had learned how to breed and grow farm animals, and they had learned how to make charcoal. The result was the rebirth of the American barbecue.

The weekly barbecue took place Saturday night, before the weekly church services. The camp was seeming more and more like the American world—before.

The whole camp ate together, Saturday nights. The unlucky centers of attention were slaughtered outside of camp, and toted in on poles. By mid-afternoon, the meat would be rotating over glowing coals, with children vying for the privilege of turning the spits. By dusk, the barbecue smell was everywhere.

The week's produce was flaunted. Corn. Peas. Beans. Melons, when some amateur farmer got lucky and drained his or her plot of land properly. And, of course, citrus fruit.

"But no tomatoes," Sigmund mourned. "I have not found anybody who can raise tomatoes."

"Has it occurred to you," Bo couldn't resist baiting him, "that it might be the land, and not the people?"

"The land? What's the matter with this land?" Sigmund glared like a member of the Florida JayCees, which he was.

"Maybe tomatoes need cold weather, or something. Why don't you have a contest?"

Sigmund's face lit up. "Brilliant," he trilled. "Absolutely brilliant, Colonel!" As he trotted away, Sigmund was already writing on his clipboard.

Next day, the posters were all over camp. They were printed on the backs of old circulars announcing a bazaar and flea market to be held in the gym and parking lot of Star of the Sea School, December 29th. Plenty of bargains, food, entertainment and prizes were promised, but the war had intervened.

Sigmund's appeal was more direct, more urgent. CAN YOU GROW TOMATOES? the top line demanded. WIN PRIZES— lavish rewards of food and clothing—3 GARMENTS OF YOUR CHOICE FOR YOU OR FAMILY MEMBERS plus EMERGENCY MEDICAL KIT and 4 SEED PACKETS dazzled the readers.

The next weeks were rife with ambition, suspicion, paranoia, and despair. Everybody had their plot of land, or roughly made wooden flat, studded hopefully with little stakes to tie their tomato plants to.

"Tomatoes sure seem to be *fussy* plants," Bo commiserated with a woman who'd been front runner in the contest—until a heavy rainstorm had turned her darlings into piles of mold.

"And I remember when all I knew about the goddamn things was that Weight Watchers let you have all you wanted," she wailed.

There had only been four packets of tomato seeds to begin with, and they would shortly run out altogether.

It was May, it was Saturday night. Everybody had their favorite place to eat, their favorite folks to eat with. Bo sarcastically called his group the power elite. The Commander, the General, the Quartermaster and wife, the Drillmaster and himself, the Exec. They ate against the wall of Sigmund's biggest supply building. The ground was soft, the grass long, and there weren't too many scuttling creatures.

This night, the Carnes family wasn't eating. They were strutting with studied casualness across the barbecue area, holding a square of cloth between them. The cloth contained something heavy and lumpy. Sara, Tom, and Belinda Carnes stepped daintily over playing children and men tossing dice in the dust. They paid no attention to nursing mothers, or old folks gumming at corn on the cob. They pressed the corners of the cloth together, and looked smug.

The Commander was sitting Indian-style, pretending to eat

some grits. She leaned forward courteously. "Mr. and Mrs.— Carnes?"

"Yes, ma'am." The Carnes clan nodded in turn at every member of the junta. "We'd—uh—like to show you something."

"Is it something red and round and edible?" All heads turned to Juanita, and then to Tom Carnes, who, with false demureness, pulled a spectacular, ripe tomato out of the bedsheet.

After the celebration, the bestowing of prizes, and the eating, Juanita leaned up to Tom Carnes's ear. "I knew a real farmer could do it."

Tom spat into the fire. "Mph. These folks don't know shit from Shinola, comes to growing stuff." He leaned close, and spoke low. "Most crops, manure is good fertilizer."

"Yeah?"

"Tomatoes, they don't like it. You got to use wood ash, with this kind of soil."

"Ah." Juanita gave the Carneses an encouraging smile. "I guess you could run classes for everybody. Show them how it's done."

"We could *sell* tomatoes, if we keep quiet," Belinda said. Sara boxed the teenager's ears.

"Sure, we'll help out. Now I got a question," Tom looked the General right in the eye. "How'd you know about our tomatoes?"

"I, ah, wander around outside camp a lot, Tom. Checking security. You did a good camouflage job, but not good enough to fool somebody who's looking for booby traps."

A team from Squad Four had won extra points from Sigmund for boating an entire mimeograph machine from the wreckage of the Inverness Regional Junior High School, across the lake. The Quartermaster printed a whole tomato-growing guide, but he was running low on ink. At the bottom of the tomato bulletin was the following: IF YOU ARE APPROACHED BY STRANGERS LOOKING FOR THE CAMP, REMEMBER THESE IMPORTANT RULES.

1) Do *not* bring them directly to camp.

2) Do *not* tell them the camp location, or anything else about it.
3) *Do* ask who they are and where they come from.
4) *Do* come directly to the nearest patrol or security station and notify them of the strangers' presence.

X

1.

Bo figured the Intelligence Officer had been about fifteen during the war, but he was giving a good briefing anyway.

"... regional report first, if I may." The young man looked around obsequiously. He slapped the hand-carved pointer smartly against the five-foot map, and Bo craned to see the target of its tip. "Since the smallpox scare of last October, we've made reconnaissance sweeps, and we can set a fairly exact perimeter for the activites of the occupying power in the state of Florida. Starting on a west-east line from Yankeetown," he tapped an inlet on the Gulf Coast, "to Ormond," he tapped a spot on the Atlantic Coast, a bit further north, "*no* enemy activity has been spotted by our listening posts as we move north of town."

"Am I to understand, Lieutenant, that no enemy air activity has been noted south of your line?" Juanita drawled.

The young man blushed. "Uh, well, of course, ma'am," he stammered, "there have been overflights... low-flying aircraft."

"And what have we done about these aircraft, Lieutenant?"

His face went blank. He had not noticed the dreaded General, sitting in the third row. His Captain rescued him.

"Aside from tracking them, in cooperation with other American camps, General," the black woman said, "we have stepped up our camouflage activities. Lieutenant?" she nodded, and he launched into an elaborate description of the imitation forests, imitation ruins and imitation hills that covered the whole camp.

"Very thorough, Lieutenant," Juanita eased up. "Now, where would you establish the new Russki line?"

"East-west from Gainesville, and pulling back every day."

"Your experience in Newberry would be a good example, General," the Captain added. "Sometimes they're gone— north—for weeks before any of our people can verify it." She was a sharp one, this woman.

"Ladies and gentlemen, I have a theory," Juanita said very softly. Christ, more of her Bache meeting techniques, Bo thought. She told me about this one . . . talk very softly and make everybody crane to hear you. You dominate the meeting. "My theory is that, smallpox or no smallpox, the occupying power is pulling back in Florida. Because their supply lines have run thin. Because their personnel is running thin. They tried to occupy territory further south, and have found they *just can't hold it*. Perhaps this is just," she shrugged her shoulders ruefully, "woman's intuition." The crowd laughed appreciatively. "But if I am right, if I am *right*," she pounded the chair for emphasis, "then we have seen the first contraction of the Russian occupying forces, the first acknowledgement on their part that they can no longer ride the American tiger."

She looked around the table, and up and down the rows of chairs. They were with her, all right. "And, my fellow officers, we are here in the right time and right place to start sending them home where they belong." She ended quietly, and sat down. The meeting applauded.

A Captain Medford waved his hand. "Interesting you should say that, General! Latin Quarter—that's New Orleans— captured some Russki records. They said they couldn't keep up the railbeds in Florida. Too much 'vandalism,' to use their words."

"A combination of Florida elements and our sabotage, I hope," the Commander said. "Perhaps I noticed something in the, uh, General's speech you all did not. She told us that the Russkies have not attacked this camp only because it's too much trouble." She glared at the younger woman.

"No reflection on the camp, Commander." The blonde smiled vixenishly. "I call it great good luck."

The rest of the meeting was devoted to planning for the Day, the uprising. After two hours, Juanita rose again to take command. "I think we've done a good job here tonight. I now realize that New Hampshire is expecting too much of us in some ways." (Sighs.) "And not enough in other ways. (Sighs of satisfaction.) Now, I'm sure you've all heard the rumor. About what day is the Day. The Day, the uprising, is set for the Fourth of July."

The meeting broke into wild applause and cheers. They spilled outside, to spread the news.

By dawn, everybody knew. Bo saw a young mother rocking her infant to sleep, to the tune of "The Star Spangled Banner."

"How the hell are we supposed to attack in two months?" Bettina raged. It was May 6th. "It'll take us twelve days to march a hundred and twelve miles—under the best conditions. And how do we move supplies? It'll take weeks to build enough carts."

"Transportation will be handled by . . . outside sources, Commander."

"What sources? The chariots of the Gods?" The three of them had stayed behind in the briefing room, and now Bo was caught between the women. Bettina was livid. "You propose to send twenty-five hundred men with arms and supplies overland, on roads that are shot to hell, probably booby-trapped . . ."

"I propose, Commander, to send every able-bodied person who wishes to engage the enemy. And every non-able-bodied person who wishes to go along in a support function."

The Commander sat down, panting with rage. "I give up. Do whatever the hell you want. Just don't associate me with this massacre."

For a moment, fury lit Juanita's eyes. He thought he almost saw flames behind them. Then she got up, picked up the pretentious pointer the Intelligence Lieutenant used, and tapped it on the big map.

Tap, tap. There they were, near Dunellon, on the east end of Lake Rousseau. The camp. Tap. Now the pointer was in the middle of the lake. It slid west across the lake and down the river to the Gulf. A thirteen-mile march, in the wrong direction.

Tap, tap. The pointer moved out into the Gulf, out and northbound, around Cedar Key.

"A boat? A ship? We've got a ship?" Bettina was electric with excitement.

"Valdosta's fifty miles inland!" Bo protested. The pointer glided up the Gulf Coast to Suwannee Sound, and slid scratchily up the path of the Suwannee River, north into the root of the Florida peninsula. At Ellaville, their old campsite, it stopped, tapped again, and turned north on a faint waterline that Bo remembered as the Georgia Withlacoochee. And the Georgia Withlacoochee flowed right by Valdosta, just east of the town of Quitman.

"Where the Carnes family comes from. So they must . . ."

". . . know Valdosta," Juanita finished crisply. "Why did you think I was so hot to save them? And where do you think we got this?" She flipped up the map of the Florida-Georgia area, and there was a block-by-block plan of Valdosta. Deliberately, she put the pointer back on the easel, and sat down.

Bettina was subdued. "How many will this boat take?"

"The whole fucking camp, Commander. So you see, we *can* use the human wave."

June was passing, and they were waiting for further supplies. Not many people beyond the immediate council knew they were also waiting for a ship. They got a few deliveries by air drop. Guns, bayonets, drugs, grenades. They marveled over the grenades. There were some new ones, shaped like dumb-bells, that were hard to throw but went off with a really big kick.

But the last week of June, other vital supplies were still missing. "They're on the boat, I'm sure," Bettina grumbled. "And damned if I'm asking that cunt one more question."

"Ship," Bo corrected automatically.

As the day of judgment grew nearer, Juanita was growing more and more remote. She seemed to be enveloping herself in a shell, pulling back into it. He had made love to her, and she did not resist, but did not respond. She had started prowling, nighttimes, slipping away with a knife, a rifle, and binoculars.

Bo and Bettina were sharing a few slugs of the ever-reliable corn whiskey, though he wondered if it was good for her, in her condition. After his third drink, he told Bettina about the woman's withdrawal.

"She's preparing to die, in her way. As I am, in mine." She raised a hand to shut him up, and took another swallow. "Let's not pretty it up with lies, or sugar it up with false sentiment," she said. "I would have been a goner in March, if she hadn't ordered the doc to save me. So at least we know she keeps her promises."

"I never doubted that."

"I did. I doubted a lot about her. But one thing I spotted from the start: she will welcome death. A lot more than I will."

"Oh, my God," he groaned.

"I *will* live to see the uprising." She poured a few more ounces from jug into her cup, and signaled for his. "Here's to the Day." They saluted each other, clicked mugs, and drank.

"Sometimes I think...about the way my life would have been..." he brooded.

"Should have been, if the nation hadn't acted like a fool," she said crossly.

"Should have been, then. She always tells me 'don't look back.' I still can't think of her as a Barbara."

"That's her name? Hm. Aha. The Jensens, you know them, the guy who wears the fedora with the feather in the band? And no teeth? And his son-in-law, they live over by the big food shed. They've got a little dog, an old cocker spaniel they've brought with them from home. Old Man Jensen told me, the other day his boy was calling the dog while Her Mightiness passed by, and she froze in her tracks. He says the dog's name is Buffy."

"Barbara—Buffy. *Not* an impressive name for our Five Star Blondie."

Malice gleamed in the old woman's smile. "Why don't you try it out next time you're screwing her?" Then it faded. "Aww. I'm sorry," she reached out and patted his hand. "She was probably a very nice Buffy. A good wife, and mother to her children. Just like I," she sighed wearily, "I was kindly old Aunt Betty, back from her wandering days to retire in the old home town."

"There's nobody here that didn't get zapped, somehow."
"God's truth. 'Nother drink?"

2.

Myron Jackson was conducting troop exercises with great gusto. As usual.

"You're a Nazi, Myron," Bettina told him. Myron's idea of troop exercises was four hours of calisthenics in the Florida summer sun. Five hours sneaking through the jungle, starting at midnight. Six hours of hand-to-hand and bayonet drill, followed by a brisk trot through the swamp.

"They're not going to make a fool of me this time." To Myron, the Russian "they" was interchangeable with the Vietnamese.

Myron was leading the drill for Squad Seven, as usual. In the other squads there were too many amateurs, and Myron would get apoplectic when the amateurs couldn't recite the five ways to camouflage a gun emplacement, or the four ways to soundlessly load and aim a mortar. He left their training to other, more patient, veterans.

Today, Myron assigned his pets—mostly Marine and Ranger alumni—taking the beach.

As Myron announced with gusto that today they would take the beach, Cpl. Robert DeBaille objected.

"Sir? There's no beach in Valdosta. Wouldn't we be better off..."

Enraged, Myron ordered Cpl. DeBaille to "do the lake, on the double!"—the most dreaded punishment. You had to make a complete circuit of Lake Rousseau, and be back within five hours. A seventeen-mile march, most of it through swampy land with the mosquitoes they called Florida Eagles. No way to fake it, either. They had lost three men doing the lake, but found only one body.

Cpl. Robert DeBaille trudged off with resignation. As soon as he was out of sight, Myron grumpily changed Squad Seven's exercise of the day to quietly sneaking up on the enemy.

Myron was standing at attention by the waterline, happily identifying soldiers who snuck too noisily by name, as they tried to slither past him undetected. Noisy Sneakers had to start the obstacle course over again. Suddenly, one of the Squad Seven men bolted upright, breaking all the rules, and yelled "Holy shit!" He pointed to the lake.

Myron looked behind him. Rounding the bend in the lake, aiming for camp, was a boat. A *big* boat. A big, multi-deck ferry, completely festooned and camouflaged with palm fronds, top and sides. Peeking through palms, at the prow of the *Chesapeake Belle* was Cpl. Robert DeBaille. "Yoo-hoo, Major" he trilled, and waved cheerily.

Myron was too astonished to order a suitable punishment.

The *Chesapeake Belle* was under command of a Coast Guard Captain, manned by a mixed Coast Guard and Navy crew assembled from all over the country. She had been hidden from Russian eyes in Maine, and refitted to run as silently as a forty-year-old ferry could. She was equipped with radar, sonar, loran, and four elaborate radios.

She did *not* carry guns.

"I'm a people-mover, not a fighter," was the standard comment of Captain Gerhardt. "Besides, we'll be close enough to shore you can walk it, if I get sunk."

"Your gear is supposed to prevent that little problem," Juanita chided.

"Shit, yes. I can spot a cockroach at five thousand yards." The Captain's good humor was unruffled.

As a formal debut into camp, and the war, Juanita proposed to the Captain that they re-christen the *Belle*.

After sunset, the camp maintained a blackout. Windows were shaded, fires had to be under cover, and everyone usually kept to their quarters. But word of the ceremony spread, and virtually the whole camp stood by the shore, in silence and darkness.

Bo led Bettina out of her cabin, saying he wanted her help with something. It was to be a surprise. Once again, the fragile feel of her wasted arm startled him, and he had to help her walk smoothly. The crowd parted silently before them, and the moon came out from behind a cloud. They could see the ship, its Captain and crew lined up smartly by the makeshift dock in the camouflaged cove.

"What's the surprise party, Beauregard?" she muttered between clenched teeth.

"You're re-christening the ship, Commander. There's some feeling that *Chesapeake Belle* doesn't have the correct military tone, if you get my meaning."

"And what the hell am *I* going to call it?"

"Anything you want. Just as long as you name it after the father of our country, or our first president, or the guy who's on the dollar bill."

As they drew near, Bettina pulled herself erect, shook off Bo's hand, and strode forward. She saluted the crew, who saluted smartly in return. While Bettina's hand was up, Juanita stepped out from behind the line, so the old woman didn't have to give her a separate salute. At least, that was what Bo guessed.

The General was holding a bottle, a Champagne bottle, fully corked and sealed! Taylor New York State, it said.

"Commander Shanahan, it's our privilege to be here, to witness the christening of this vessel. Your pleasure, ma'am." She thrust out the bottle. The Commander grabbed it by the neck, stepped up to the battered steel prow, and yelled at the top of her gravelly voice.

"I hereby christen this ship—the U.S.S. *George Washington!*" With a vigorous whack, she splintered the bottle and the crowd cheered.

Bo saw her sag, and slipped behind to prop her up. "Waste of good booze," she muttered, drooping in his arms.

While the camp celebrated, he quietly picked the Commander of the camp up like a baby, and carried her to her bed. She did not protest.

It was the twentieth of June.

"We've got the troops, as well trained as they'll ever be." Myron nodded back. "We've got a pretty good supply of arms, particularly those suited to hand-to-hand combat." Sigmund nodded back at the Executive Officer. "We've got the means of transport." Captain Gerhardt nodded back. "Today." Bo looked around the table challengingly. In his role as Executive Officer, he was conducting this Staff conference. The Commander was unable to attend. "Today, we're here to agree on the final battle plan." He paused.

"Our maps of the city of Valdosta are based on eye-witness information from natives of the area, and from General Mallinson's reconnaissance. That information is now six months old, so we must be prepared for some surprises.

"Let's first consider what could go *wrong*, in our attack plan."

The next forty-five minutes was filled with everything from more mines on the town perimeters and advance patrols, to ground-level radar, and other possible snares. Juanita was silent. When he felt the speakers were becoming repetitive, he interrupted. "Thank you, officers. I think that's a good overview of the possible booby-traps and unpleasant surprises that may await us. Now, let's turn our attention to *solutions*. Corporal, let's go back in the minutes, to the first issue raised."

The stenographer flipped back the pages, and read in a flat, mechanical tone. "Captain Walgreen: What if they've spotted us coming up the river?"

Eleven exhausting hours later, they had not coped with all the possibilities, but Bo adjourned the conference.

It was the twenty-fourth of June.

Bo staggered to the Commander's cabin, to report on the meeting. She was awake, alert and interested, but not in any condition to make command decisions.

He slogged back to the cabin he shared with Juanita. He saw a speck of light peek through the blackout curtains, and cringed at the thought of her criticisms, Instead, she got off the bed, hugged him and beamed. "You did that *very* well. Congratulations."

Bo glowed all over. The woman was constantly surprising him, and, this time, in the nicest way. "Yeah?" he said, fishing for more compliments.

"You were tough. Concise. You had your eye on the end goal all the time. You kept them moving without discouraging free thinking. That's leadership."

He almost drooled with pleasure.

"In fact, Colonel, I'd say that you were the ideal officer to lead the attack on Valdosta."

He sobered instantly. "I'm a Lieutenant Colonel, and I'm second in command."

"You've been promoted. And you know what I mean. Bettina's dying and I'm . . . probably going to take one chance too many." She sat down on the bed's edge, her legs folded. "I'm not blind to what I've become, despite what Bettina may think." He winced. "Yeah. I'm bloodthirsty. I want revenge. Which is risky." She looked like a Barbara now. A mother, giving advice, with an earnest air. "So after Valdosta, you've got to lead."

"God help me."

"I believe He will. Anyway, in God we trust, haven't you heard?"

"Sure," he said. "All others pay cash."

She laughed, and he laughed, like joke-drunk teenagers.

On June twenty-fifth, again under his direction, the Command council finished planning for eventualities. The Commander was present, but contributed little.

Bo escorted the last of the council out of the big hut, swathed with camouflaging plants. When he turned around, he saw Juanita carrying the Commander as he had done, one arm under her shoulders, the other under her knees. Muscles bulged from the younger woman's shoulders and forearms. He followed them across the compound, and opened the door.

She laid Bettina gently on her bed. The old woman opened her eyes, now sunken in her skull. "Thanks, Buffy," she whispered with a fine malice.

They went out the door and closed it. "That damned dog!" Juanita said furiously. "They called me Buffy when I was a kid. I *hate* it. Even worse than 'Bobbie.'"

3.

They were eating outdoors, because a brisk sunset breeze had banished mosquitoes and midges. Bo gingerly skirted around the subject.

"What you're trying to find out is, how did I know about the boat," she said.

"Ship."

"The ship, and other things I never told you. Right?"

"Right."

"Simple. I have two radio identities. Spic chick is for the stuff that's not top secret. Betty's Place is our open camp call sign, too. For stuff that's not vital."

She was drawing in the sandy dust. It was the outline of somebody in a floor-length robe, with big sleeves and shoulder-length hair. Now she drew wings on the figure.

"An angel?"

"Malakh-ha-Mavet—the Angel of Death."

"Angel of—that's what you told Ferguson . . ."

"That's what I am. The Hebrew angel of death is Azriel. That's my code name." She gave a sour smile. "Don't you think I've earned it?"

"Don't start." He waved a denying hand in front of his face.

"OK," she said crisply. "Azriel is the name you use to get the hot stuff direct from Lost River. Nobody else should respond to the name. If they do, close down."

"What about the radio operators? Are you sure they're secure?"

"Threaten them with death. It works. You spell Azriel A-Z-R-I-E-L. It's the code for the whole thing. Assault Azriel. And this camp is Galilee."

"Who goes?"

"Everybody goes."

"Oh shit."

"Asshole," she snarled, and he was afraid of her again. "This is make or break. I wasn't kidding about the human wave. It's the only way we'll make it. We can cut through their front lines all right." She leaned back, and he breathed again. "But the only way we'll *hold* Valdosta is, whenever, wherever we cut through their lines, a wave of furious humanity— furious *American* humanity—runs over the barricades and wipes them out."

"For Christ's sake, why?"

"The Russkies are demoralized already. Their grip on some of the territories is weakening. Listen to their radio, you'll hear. More American crops being grown, less being turned over to the Commissars. More people vanishing from the work drafts. Slipping out of the labor camps. We're getting them here—over a hundred in the last month. Russki soldiers deserting—*deserting* in a foreign land, where they know the locals may kill them."

"Yeah, great. We've probably got some here."

"I've been keeping an eye on that. We've had six, but only one made any attempt to contact . . . home base."

"You dealt with him?"

"Yeah," she smiled ruefully. "He, ah, sleeps with the fishes, as they say."

"Thank God we don't have to drink lake water. Why haven't you told me any of this?"

"Until now, you didn't need to know. I've been doing advance planning. After the assault, tight security will be a waste of time. One way or the other."

"OK, OK, no hard feelings," he waved his hands in a way that showed there *were* hard feelings. "So why the human wave?"

"It scares the shit out of them that's why. And we need to have them terrorized, to make our point. Remember, they used it on the Germans, in the World Wars."

"Mm. And then the Chinese used it on them, at Khabarovsk."

"Where do you think we got the idea? All the Chinese had was people, when the Border Wars began. They used 'em."

"You really believe the Russkies are losing their grip? That the army of occupation is softening up?"

"Mm. And they're just beginning to realize it. Plus, they've got to have heard we're planning something for a Glorious Fourth." She rubbed her hands together gleefully. "I can't wait."

"Why are you in such a hurry to die?" He spoke very softly, and she froze. Moments passed. They listened to voices murmuring, guitars strumming, and the eternal chorus of frogs and crickets.

"I already did." She wouldn't look at him. "This isn't me. At least, that's what I tell myself, to excuse what I have done." She shifted uneasily, and he felt a lump rise in his throat. "When I think about what Juanita has done, to stay alive, to get revenge, I know it *can't* be me. and whoever she is, this Juanita will burn a long time in hell. Shit," she lightened her mood and her voice, "I guess I'm just crazy."

Bo wrapped his arms around her, and repeated what he'd once heard a Bible-thumping evangelist shout. "God understands even more than we hope He does."

On the twenty-ninth of June, a general camp assembly was called. The Commander watched from her porch. The rest of the camp sat in darkness, but the speakers were lit by kerosene lanterns, under cover of the largest tent.

"This is the order of the day for the thirtieth of June." Juanita was using a bullhorn, speaking urgently. "All troops will board the *George Washington* starting at 1400 hours. Starting at 1700 hours, all camp personnel who wish to participate in the uprising may board. You will be . . ."

A cheer drowned out the rest of the sentence, and lasted many minutes. The General spoke again. "That's right. Everybody gets to go. To see the Russkies get beat, and to see to it they *are* beaten." More cheers. "All personnel aboard will be equipped with handguns, rifles, grenades, or other weapons. You will be expected to do your part when you are called on. You must stick together, and move together, as you are ordered. Our objective is to seize the fort at Valdosta and *hold* it, in one day. To do it, we need all of you.

"Once we have swept into the town, with the troops leading, it's your job to see it's held. You will be assigned stations you must hold, and jobs you must do. Majors Jackson and Wallberg will be in charge of arming you and giving you specific instructions." She lowered the bullhorn and cleared her throat.

"This is the day we have waited for since the United States was defeated. This is the day we start to win again." She ended simply and quietly.

Instead of a cheer, somebody in the back of the crowd began to sing. "O-oh say can you see . . ."

By the line "what so proudly we hail," the entire assembly was singing along, at the top of their lungs. Bo and Juanita bellowed the anthem directly into each other's face. On the other side of the field the Commander was trying to sing, but her crying interfered.

"Oh say does that star-spangled banner still wa-ave
O'er the land of the free
And the home of the brave."

Even Myron Jackson was sobbing and laughing at the same time. He grabbed the bullhorn, and yelled "Dis-missed!" but he hiccoughed in the middle.

By dawn, sobriety had returned. The camp was still and subdued. In every tent, cabin, and hut, debate raged.

"You can't go. What about the baby?"

"The baby comes with me."

"No!"

"All right, I'll leave the baby behind with old Susy Bullitt."

"You'll never see him again."

"Then I'll take the baby. But I'm going."

"You're seventy years old!"

"Not too old to shoot a rifle."

"Too old to run."

"Who's running?"

"The Major said you load this through the handle. How?"

"The butt. Pull this little thing..."

"Aha! It holds bullets!"

"Six. After you fire the automatic six times, slip this cartridge out again, and reload."

"Only six? Maybe you'd better tell me about grenades."

"How many are going?" The Commander was stronger today. She sat up in bed, nibbling on bread and butter.

"Easier to say how many are staying. Looks like less than a hundred."

Bettina dropped her slice of bread, and coughed. "Jeeesus Christ! Out of nine thousand?"

"Nine thousand, six hundred, ninety-two, as of yesterday noon. Here, eat." Bo picked up the bread and waved it temptingly in front of her mouth.

"Do they know what to do?"

"We worked out a directive... hope it covers most of the possibilities. Sigmund's going to distribute it once we're on board."

"The cruise of the *Chesapeake Belle*," she pondered. "Ship of fools."

Bo sat down on the bed. "Look, *I* think it's crazy, and *you* think it's crazy. But we're operating only on what we know, what we've seen. I think the High Command has probably got it all together. And so far, the lady you call the zombie seems to know what she's doing."

"So you're going on faith."

"Guess you could put it that way."

"Oh, well." She leaned back against the wall, crumbs and grease at the corners of her mouth. "I believe she does mean to wipe out Russkies, and I'll go along with that. What the hell."

"What the hell." Bo looked through the cracked window, and saw the light was failing. "Time to go. Wish me luck, and I'll be back to tell you all about it."

Bettina grabbed his face between two wasted hands, and planted a dry, crumby kiss on his forehead. He kissed her in return, slipped his rifle strap over his left shoulder, and departed.

Juanita slid around the corner of the porch and came in.

"You should have told him. Ready?"

"He'd have screamed and hollered to beat the band, and I'm in no condition for an argument. Ready."

There was a kit bag by the bed. It was faded maroon, with white piping and straps, and said "Kissimmee Varsity." Juanita hooked it over her right arm, swaddled the Commander in bedclothes, and hoisted her with a grunt.

XI

1.

The *George Washington*'s engines started up tentatively, one at a time. They were muffled and baffled as much as could be, but they still sounded obscenely loud if you were the nervous sort. There were small whines as different systems cut in. Radar. Sonar. The *George Washington* might not be a stealthy craft, but she was equipped to find out if anybody else was in the area.

Amazingly, they departed on time. It wasn't yet fully dark, though there was hardly any twilight time to speak of in the sub-tropics.

The small band left behind—almost all elderly, crippled, diseased, or pregnant—waved frantically. The one-legged man who cast off lines from the dock was crying. The *George*, as her crew and passengers were already calling her, moved more smoothly as the engines slipped into their rhythms.

It seemed only minutes later that the lake narrowed to the river running to the Gulf. Those who had "done the lake" on foot cursed nostalgically.

The river passage was scary, if you didn't know how sonar worked. Sometimes it seemed they came so near to shore, on one bank or the other, that they would run aground. Then it seemed to get lighter, and if you looked west, you could see moonlight glinting on the waters of the Gulf of Mexico.

The moment she was clear of the delta river mud, the *George* turned hard right, so hard some people were rocked on their feet, or rolled over in sleep.

"We're sticking close to the shore, all right."

"God, yes. Look at that!" The speaker pointed to the ruins of a high-rise apartment house. It was reduced to a ragged stump, some seven stories tall, with white brick and glass rubble lying about its foot. In front, enragingly eternal, a perfect white sand beach glowed in the night.

"Good as a Goddamned cruise ship," Bo chortled. He was using night glasses to view the wreckage. The high-rise had suffered a mighty fall, obliterating several more humble dwellings as it died. "Why would they bomb here?"

"They didn't. Must have been a storm."

"A storm? Knock down a steel-frame high-rise?"

"If the sump pumps aren't running to keep water out of the foundations, and the pilings rot, and nobody maintains the bulkhead... it doesn't matter how strong the frame is."

"Oh. Huh." He thought about it. "I wonder what happened to..." he trailed off.

"The Empire State Building?" she taunted. "Let us say the elements never got the chance to destroy it. But the Empire State Building was anchored in solid granite."

Silently, he put the glasses back to his eyes. As they chugged north, the buildings got smaller, the land swampier. "Think we'll make the Suwannee by dawn?"

"On schedule so far. There's the next river."

"The Wacca—"

"Waccasassa."

"It'll never make it on the hit parade."

"Next landmark is Cedar Key." Sure enough, they were gently turning northwest, following the shore. "And Cedar Key Bridge."

The bridge was a refreshing sight. It was whole, and trim of line, and closed. Unfortunately, the messy hulk of a half-sunk tanker blocked the center channel under it. The General and the Captain looked at each other, and he ordered a course around the key.

"Fucking recon..." she gritted her teeth.

"Maybe they never surveyed this part."

She turned around and waved her hands, lit by the red lights of the ship's bridge. "They had distinct orders to do so," she hissed. "Oh, God, nothing else goes right. Why should this?"

They wove their way between Cedar and its subsidiary

keys, and pulled in tight to the shoreline again, running at minimum depth.

The triple-deck ferry wove in and out, dutifully following the commands of its electronic eyes and feelers. The coves, bays, and swampy points of land looked as if only animals had ever lived there.

There was a deep-throated roar, and the ship leapt forward. Juanita whipped across the top deck, back into the bridge. The Captain and ship's Exec were bending over an intricate radar screen. They made way for the General.

"Aircraft at two-three-three, altitude eleven thousand, traveling at four hundred, approx."

"Russki recon?"

"A prop plane, following the coast. Probably."

The *George Washington* headed for the nearest inlet at top speed, the engines making every part of the ship vibrate in sympathy.

"Full stop. All engines off!" the Captain barked, but not soon enough. The *George* slid ahead on her own momentum, and beached with a sickening, gummy thud. Bo heard a chain of smaller thuds as people and objects fell and rolled. Babies began to wail, but were muzzled.

"Let's hope," he prayed aloud, "they haven't got heat-detection cameras."

"Scanners are the real problem." Juanita's eyes never left the screen. "By the time they get a photo developed, we'll be gone."

"I'd rather they not know we were *ever* here."

All lights and motors off, cemented to the shore, all the *George Washington* could do was keep her eyes and ears—human and technological—open. She was draped with fresh camouflage greenery for her voyage, and her twin radar dishes spun comically over the fronds. Nobody saw the joke except Bettina, who sat on the top stern deck and looked at the sky.

The plane, a lumbering four-engine Ilyushin, beat its way ponderously overhead. It could be clearly seen and identified, even without glasses.

"I don't see a radar dome."

"But who knows what they've developed since the war," another voice chimed in.

"Not that." Juanita pulled the glasses away from her eyes. The unfamiliar roar faded south. "Now we've got to get this mother off the beach."

The Captain sighed and went back inside. "Attention, attention," the loudspeaker squawked. It was the kind of loudspeaker used to announce when the next ferry would leave, where the rest rooms and bar were located. It did not sound military. "All hands—that is everybody—move to the stern of the ship. We must lighten the prow. Thank you."

Boots and bare feet and homemade sandals plodded to the stern, which was jam-packed with humanity in moments. Quietly and cooperatively, they stacked themselves up like cordwood. The loudspeaker crackled again. "Thank you. Everybody hold on." Before the message was finished, the old diesel engines kicked on with a roar, churning the water into deep whirlpools.

"Oh, God," the Captain begged, "please make this work. I don't want to have to get out and push." He looked eagerly at the shore, just a couple of yards beyond his prow, and hoped to see it recede, but it didn't. The trees stayed the same stubborn distance away. The engines made horrific noise, stirred up vast quantities of mud and threatened to break loose from their moorings. No go.

Captain Gerhardt turned to tell his men to shut them down. The next logical step was to order all the able-bodied men off, to lighten the draft. But the crazy blonde General yelled "Keep 'em running!" and grabbed the loudspeaker mike.

"Everybody jump!" she shrieked over the engine roar. "Everybody jump up and down, in unison." She dropped the mike, ran out on the aft deck, and proceeded to leap up in the air with astonishing, adolescent agility. The people crushed together stared through one jump. Two jumps. Then they got the idea, and the top deck joined in, in ragged time. As they tightened it up, the ship began to lurch with each jump.

Then a few kids from the lower decks ran up, got the picture, and led the lower decks, jumping in sync.

One—thud! Two—crash! Three-bam! The prow of the *George Washington* shot up out of the water so hard and fast her screws began to eat mud, then she started backwards. People howled and held on to each other. Thank God they had wire netting around each deck, to hold the camouflage and, now, the passengers.

The ship careened backwards. By the time the Captain could get his mouth to work again, she was trucking off at five knots, and leaving a messy wake behind her prow.

"All engines—slow!" He cleared his throat. "Port engines, reverse."

With comic dignity, like a duchess who has taken a pratfall and now must gather her poise, the *George Washington* stopped, turned her nose toward the Gulf, and glided back to open water.

The Captain fixed the ship's Exec with a glazed stare. "High Command told me that woman was crazy," he said. "But she gets *results*."

"Sure am glad I didn't have to get out in that water," the Exec nodded vigorously. "I saw a man once, got bit by one of those water moccasins they got down here?" His drawl made it clear his own home was not much further north, but nervous relief kept him chattering. "His leg swole up like the Goodyear blimp. Turned blue. They wheeled him into intensive care and..."

"Thank you, thank you, Sam." The Captain forestalled any more grisly details. "Check sonar. Hard right, soon as we have enough clear draft."

They made a hard right, and then a soft right, into the meandering delta of the Suwannee River. The quality of the night sky was changing. Visibility was worse than at dusk. The Captain saluted Juanita, then realized she wore no insignia. Not even a proper uniform. "Ma'am, we're running behind schedule. Still in the delta, and dawn's coming."

"I see that." Her voice was edgy. "When do you think you can make Manatee?" It was their scheduled stop for the day.

"It's fifteen miles!"

"How long? At top speed?" Top speed was suicide where you didn't have accurate charts. And besides, at top speed you left enough wake for the Russkies to spot from the air, hours later.

The Captain sighed. "All ahead flank," he told the bridge.

They made Manatee at 0723 hours, when it had been full light for an hour. Everyone the Captain could see had stood anxiously on the deck, peering at the sky, the jungle and the river ahead, but they had seen nothing. They pulled into an inlet—slowly and delicately, this time—and shut down.

Bo was trying to find (a) Juanita, and (b) a place to sleep away the daylight hours. He found Bettina instead, wrapped in her coverlet, her head pillowed on her kit bag. She looked like the very death.

"What the hell?" he yelled, waking the other twenty-odd occupants of what had been the women's lounge of the *Chesapeake Belle*. "You're not supposed to be here," he growled into the old woman's ear. "And dammit, don't pretend to be asleep."

She opened her eyes sheepishly. "That jumping kinda tuckered me out."

"Jumping!" He smote his forehead at the folly.

"I told you. She keeps her promises, and she promised I'd see this. In person." Bettina put a mollifying hand on his arm. "Don't worry. I'm not going to kick off right away. The doc says so. And I flat *refuse* to go, until we've won."

"You need anything? Food? Drink?"

"I could use some water." She handed him her tin cup, and he went out on deck to the big distilling tanks that boiled and filtered the sinister river water. But by the time he got back to the cabin, the Commander was asleep, so he gave it to the young girl and her mother who lay next to the bulkhead. "Thanks so much, Colonel."

"You can thank me by taking care of the Commander. She's very ill."

"We know, sir. Does she have any medicine?"

"There should be some pills. In her bag, I guess. They're blue, and she should take one with a glass of water, every night."

"Got it, sir. Leave it to me." Even though she wore shorts and a T-shirt, the woman sounded military.

"Thank you, uh . . ."

"Sergeant Massey, sir." Bo grinned as he walked away.

Just behind the bridge, he saw a domed blanket propped against the bulkhead, and a pair of feet peeking out from it. He recognized the feet. "I thought only Mexicans could do that."

"Do what?" the blanket asked.

"Sleep with their knees to the chest, their backs to the wall."

"You're right. Only Mexicans *can* do it."

Bo eased down beside her, and pulled the blanket over himself, too. It was hot under there, but they snuggled side by side, and slept. It was the first of July.

2.

That night things went more smoothly. And to most, more mysteriously. The *George Washington* started running with all lights extinguished at full dusk, before 1900 hours. She felt her way up the Suwannee at a smooth, decorous pace, past Hatchbend, past the river's turn to the northwest at Branford. Tracing the edge of a giant swamp, they saw few signs of human habitation in any area.

On the bottom deck, where he'd gone to eat, Bo was tracing their progress on a small copy of the master map, for a group of the curious. They all felt it: the engines were slowing down. He looked around, and listened. When they asked him why, all he could do was shrug his shoulders. "I'll find out."

On the boat's right side—port?—he couldn't remember—people were staring out at a vast, geometric shape in the dark. The *George* was nudging up alongside it, and hit with a gentle thump. The crew attached grappling hooks and whipped out the gangplank.

"Attention, everybody," the usual loudspeaker voice said. "We are taking on additional supplies. Please leave the following areas clear, repeat, clear, of people or possessions.

"On the middle deck, clear the areas just fore and aft—that's in front and behind—of the bridge, for at least twenty

feet. New supplies of food will be stowed there by the crew."
The pounding of feet, already re-boarding with cargo, confirmed this.

"On the below deck, we are sorry, but we must ask you to clear the entire area before—in front of—the cabin and lavatories. These supplies need cover from rain or excessive heat. Thank you."

"Cover from heat and rain? Must be ammo."

"Grenades. Christ, I hope it's more grenades."

"Electronic stuff? I keep forgetting we've got it."

"Thank God they're giving us more weapons!"

"Oh, yeah? What are they giving us *less* of?"

Bo heard the dialogues, and shouldered his way to the bridge, with resignation. "Why doesn't anybody tell me what's going on around here?" he whined. Gerhardt gave him the same look back. They both glared at the General, but she was ice.

"For your information," she was biting the words out, "we have been sent these supplies at great risk, because certain of our support services have failed." She stalked around the cramped bridge. "We will not have air support, it seems. So the High Command has chosen to send us a bargain lot of freshly-stolen SAM-7's. Colonel!"

Bo braced. "Yes, ma'am!"

"Find me every man or woman who has any experience with a rocket launcher. A bazooka. A grenade gun. Anybody who knows how to load and fire something big. Good aim is not required."

"Uh, SAM-7's are?" the Captain enquired delicately.

"Heat-seekers," Bo said. "Manually-launched rockets. About five feet long, forty pounds weight." He addressed Juanita again. "What happened to our . . . ?"

"Air Force?" she glared. "They fucked up."

They were a few miles short of Luraville when dawn broke, and the *George Washington* took cover. It was July second.

Bo was climbing over the mountain of supplies, because he couldn't sleep. He estimated fifty launchers and three hundred fifty to four hundred rockets were in the pile. They looked reasonably easy to operate. Some were even packed in weird Russki crates, with helpful diagrams for assembly and operation. Freshly-stolen, indeed.

He put out a call for people who could read Russian, and a crop of teenagers appeared, shifting uneasily from foot to foot. Of course! It was a required course in the schools.

The Cyrillic alphabet looked baroque, but translated, sounded drearily familiar. "Insert the bolt through Aperture Three, holding firmly until... do not attach armpiece until this connection 'is completely... Use only Lubricant K. Other forms of lubricants will block the... When firing, brace the left leg..." They got the drift, and soon a crew of sunlight insomniacs was assembling, bolting, lubricating, and loading.

The General stalked by. Everybody but the Colonel pretended not to notice. But when she had passed they murmured to each other, careful not to let him hear. He gathered they (a) admired her, (b) were afraid of her, and (c) heard she would kill you for the least mistake.

When the SAM-7's were all assembled, and arranged neatly with their rockets, he dismissed the crew and decided to report.

Upstairs—no, topside, was that the correct term?— they were investigating the other new supplies. Cans and crates and brown burlap sacks. Tinned meat. Vegetables. All of it American.

"Don't this beat all?" a grizzled type asked. "Our food they were shipping to Russia. And we stole it back!" He cackled. Sure enough, the containers were neatly addressed, in Russian.

He slumped down in the same uncomfortable place they'd slept the day before, then rolled down on the deck, curled around the stack. At some point in the afternoon, she slipped under the blanket, too. He awoke in a sweat and, from the feel of her body wrapped around his, with an erection he could do nothing about.

Luraville to Ellaville was smooth sailing. "The problem comes when we turn onto that damn Georgia Withlacoochee." The Captain was being expansive.

"Long name for a river."

159

"Oh, there's a Florida Withlacoochee, too." Captain Gerhardt dragged his finger down the chart. "And you were on it. It's the river that feeds Rousseau."

"Withlacoochee must mean 'very useful river we like to live beside and travel on,'" Bo joked.

"It means 'river we don't know the depth of, and hope to Christ this old barge can navigate up.'"

At Ellaville, the *George Washington* slowed down to a snail's pace.

The Georgia Withlacoochee was more impressive than its name. Even now, in high summer and the dry season, it was a couple of hundred yards wide. Terra cotta colored, muddy and sluggish, but wide. Which should mean deep. The ferry daintily turned, her sonar probing, testing every footstep.

A collective sigh went up from the bridge as the sonar beepingly, pingingly told them the Georgia Withlacoochee had a nice, deep channel running down its middle. Gaining confidence with good soundings, the ship churned upstream.

Just before dawn, they squeaked under a railroad bridge that boasted gleaming patches from recent repairs.

"Hm. They've been fixing it," Juanita pondered.

"Are we crossing 31?"

"Must be," the ship's Exec answered Bo. "Georgia." They all turned to see the bridge's nether side. It was patched, too. Juanita said "hm" sourly, several times, but he didn't dare ask her why. What if the Russkies were further south than they were supposed to be?

"Where do we tie up?"

"North of Ousley, west of Remerton. Right near the old I-75."

"Interstate," he spat. "Jesus, who'd have thought it would come to this?"

"All I'm worried about is can we make it by full light." In answer, the ship's engines picked up their tempo. They were leaving a wake behind them that would be visible from any plane for some time. But it was too late to worry about it.

It was the third of July.

Exhausted by his daytime exercise and lack of sleep, Bo found the blanket he tucked behind the bridge's bolted-back door, and was asleep before he had it satisfactorily arranged.

She snuggled under it some time later. Hours? It was still dark, and he was aroused. I think I'll just celebrate this victory a little early, he chuckled to himself, and turned around to face her.

As he withdrew from her body, sweating, he could feel the ship slowing down, and see the beginnings of dawn. They were both fumbling to put their garments on again under the blanket. He kissed her. "Thank you."

She turned her head away.

The day was spent in unbearable tension and heat.

Someone had chosen the ship's destination well. It had been a small marina, or an industrial dock. There was a long dock that stretched, rather than out in the river, along the bank of the river. The *George Washington* tied up neatly, with plenty of space on the dock for passengers to disembark from every gate, fast.

Beyond the dock was a large, tin-roofed shed, in disrepair but not ruin. The cover was so narrow the trees' overhang melded with the ship's camouflage.

By the time a full crew reached the bridge in the morning, the female General was there, operating the radio alone. She was wearing earphones, writing down messages, twiddling the dials and talking gibberish into the mike.

Two minutes before 0700 hours by the bridge chronometer, she slumped back sweating, and tore off the earphones. Her look was pure despair. "Captain, please inform our forces—the assault in canceled."

"Canceled? Postponed, surely."

The woman turned and talked down to her stomach. "Canceled, Captain. It appears we've been betrayed. Please inform . . ." she raised her head and she looked ready to cry.

"Attention, all hands. Attention." Captain Gerhardt could feel his own eyes tearing. "Today's operation has been canceled, repeat, canceled, due to a breach of security."

The passengers of the U.S.S. *George Washington* woke with a hiss of horror.

"Breach of security? Who squealed?"

"They must have seen us, from that plane."

"Somebody here, somebody works for them."
"What do we do *now*?"

"What now, Ma'am?" The Captain slumped against the annunciator. He'd dressed in his last whole, proper Coast Guard uniform for the great day. The General, on the other hand, still wore ragged khaki.

"Stand by, Captain. That's the orders I get. Stand by, until they can clear us for an escape route."

Bo knew better. Defeat and inaction were not her style. The very slump of her shoulders, as she stood idly about the bridge, looked suspicious to him. If we were *really* beaten, he thought grimly, she'd kill herself.

She left the bridge to use the head, and he forced his way into the tiny steel cabin by the Captain's quarters.

"Hey..." she tried to squeeze the door shut on him, but he just glared. "Did you come here to watch me take a leak, or what?"

He kept on glaring.

"All right, all right." Her hands flew in the air mockingly. "It wasn't set for the fourth. Ever. What kind of a dumb-ass idea is it to be so predictable? To have *another* revolution on the fourth of July?"

Bo squawked weakly.

"But to the stupid," she grinned, "to the traitorous, to the Russkies—it sounds like what we *would* do, right?"

Bo whimpered again. "You think we've got Russkie agents..."

"Who knows? Who wants to take a chance? The Russkies think we attack today. When we don't, they relax."

He was galvanized. "We attack tomorrow!" he whooped, and she gouged his throat and slugged him in the gut. But he couldn't stop laughing with relief, smashed against the wall of the tiny bathroom. "Thank God, thank God."

Finally she gave up, locked him in the head and went to use another. She didn't let him out until lunch time, by which time he'd learned how to act depressed like everybody else.

"I'd better go see Bettina."
"Keep your mouth..." she grated.

"Shut. Right. I'll just see how she is."

"OK." It was appalling that she took no interest in the dying woman she had dragged along.

Bettina looked no better, no worse. She'd hobbled to and from the bathroom beyond the erstwhile ladies' lounge, eaten some cereal and powdered milk, and slept. Bo asked earnestly how she was, and assured her everything would be all right.

All right indeed. No wonder the zombie had told her not to take the pills until the final attack order was given. Bo was much more cheerful than he should have been, if the assault were really off.

Which meant it was postponed. As she'd suspected, and hoped. It was a dumb idea, to stage it for the fourth.

It was a *smart* idea, to let them think it was set for the fourth, and wait. Bettina felt the top right pocket of her tunic. There were some dark-purple pills there that the zombie assured her would change anybody into Wonder Woman for about twelve hours. She went back resolutely to eating food he didn't want, so Wonder Woman would have something to run on, and nodded politely at Bo.

Some people tried to get off the ship, but they were prevented from going any further than the wharf by Squad Seven's patrol. Myron Jackson didn't understand the order that came from the General, but by God, he knew how to obey it.

When his men (and women, although Myron didn't like to think of his troops that way) had shooed everybody back on board at nightfall, Myron reported smartly to the bridge. He was astounded to see the General smiling.

"OK, Myron. Get a good night's sleep. Tomorrow is going to be a big day."

"*The* big day, ma'am?"

The General, the Exec, the Captain, and the ship's Exec all beamed. "Why don't you just bunk down here, Major?" The General gestured to a corner lavishly lined with pillows and coverlets.

Myron also knew an order when he heard one. Taking off his smartly-ironed tunic and cap, he lay down with precision, and fell asleep with same. In the military, you always knew that if you followed orders things would take care of themselves.

3.

It wasn't even fully light yet, and the confounded P.A. system was crackling and yelling.

"Attention, all personnel. Attention. Everyone must be fully prepared to leave the ship—in formation and fully armed—in thirty minutes. Repeat, leave the ship in battle readiness in thirty minutes. Thank you."

There was a mad scramble for toilets and sinks and food, but it was performed with discipline and remarkable silence. Bo and Juanita looked on from the bridge. They were drinking some gruesome "instant coffee."

"This stuff sucks!" somebody snarled behind the radar con.

"It's Russki."

"Russkies suck."

She had gotten up, without any signal, two hours earlier, so he rose, too. The signal spread by osmosis and body electricity. Then they let Myron loose, and everybody who was officially in the U.S. Army was alerted in a matter of minutes.. So while the civilians scrambled, the troops were lining up smartly, joyfully on the lower deck by the gangplank.

After thirty minutes precisely, the General took the microphone.

"Attention, everybody. Today is the fifth of July. Today is the day." She didn't pause for cheers, and there were none. "Troops and their support will disembark first. They are already in formation.

"Volunteers, as directed, you should form yourselves in squads of roughly twenty able-bodied people each. Each squad should have at least one heavy weapon, and a few SAM-7's are still available on the middle deck. If, upon disembarking, you are separated from your squad mates, wait for them.

"Collect your rations outside the mess hall on the lower deck, and follow the regular army troops as quickly and quietly as possible. Volunteer squads will be accompanied by three communications units, so that you may be used when and where you can do the most good.

"Good luck. God bless the United States of America."

The speakers clicked off. In eerie silence, the thousands shaped themselves into orderly units. The soldiers stepped out with precision, aiming for a spot in the jungle that seemed no different from any other. As they hit it, they swung about them with machetes, clearing a trail.

"You didn't give them much information." Bo was staring down at the civilians, pitying them.

"The less they know, the better."

Bo was seized by a horrific thought. "Where's Be—the Commander?"

Juanita avoided his eye.

"She'll *die!*"

"She'll die anyway. This way, she dies *happy.* That counts. C'mon, we've got to catch up to Seven."

Grabbing canteens, M-16's, binoculars, and kit bags, they swirled across the top deck. The ship's Captain saluted smartly, and so did the bridge crew. They held the salute, with pleading expressions.

"Did you find warm bodies?" Juanita grinned.

"Yes, Ma'am!" The Captain beckoned furiously to an old man with one eye, three women, and a gaggle of small children. "McCardell here is a thirty-year Navy man. Top steam ratings. The others will help."

"I'll keep her fired up, Ma'am" the old man was sweatily earnest. "She's in top condition, so this is all the help I need." They all looked eagerly for a decision.

Juanita hiked a thumb out the door, and the ship's regular crew followed it, whooping with glee. They already had weapons of choice stashed in the deck lockers.

McCardell and the women waved good-bye, and then he began yelling at them, and they began yelling at the children.

"We'll need one man in the boiler room—make that two—to monitor the gauges!"

"Billy!" yelled a woman who wore a papoose sling.

"Wanda Debnam!" another bawled.

As the General and the Colonel left the *George Washington*, McCardell was telling an eight-year-old boy and a ten-year-old girl how to monitor steam gauges. And how to use the squawk box to get help.

They had to skirt around the volunteer squads, which were organizing quietly but far from quickly.

Sigmund Wallberg was in charge of the volunteers, haranguing them about overconsumption of vital supplies. Bo suspected Sigmund himself would bring up the rear.

Then they were passing the last of the regular troops, double-timing it through the stubbly, freshly-chopped jungle. Then they were gaining on the unmistakably-smart backs of Squad Seven, wheeling in perfect unison as they climbed the shoulders of the roadbed. It was Interstate 75, approaching Valdosta from the northwest.

They came in view of Valdosta's outer defense perimeter—the searchlight towers, fences, and barbed wire—and the leading troops fanned out, according to plan.

The Americans had calculated the Russian patrols would be most alert along the un-walled airport wing, even though they allowed for land mines, trip wires, and God knew what else. The walled areas, however, offered another peril—you couldn't be sure of what was on the other side. They had decided to do the obvious, and use the airport line as their opening wedge.

To clear the way, they would use bombs and mortars to blow everything in their path to Kingdom come.

They were supplied with American anti-tank and grenade weapons. Myron identified them as M67's and M72's and M79's. There were also a few random Russki models. But by and large, the troops insisted "the American stuff is better."

"Even if it's got to be fourteen years old?"

"And never used!" the speaker joked. "Anyway, I don't believe this stuff *is* from before the war. Looks brand new to me."

The General smiled when Myron reported this conversation to her. The ammunition for the weapons looked brand new, too.

Glancing at his watch, Bo was astounded to see they were right on schedule in reaching the town. Only a day late.

Myron was downright disappointed. He had expected only his pet elite would be able to hack it. Or, as he put it, "I don't believe anybody else in this outfit knows how to wipe their ass."

Communications were spotty. They had some walkie-talkies and field phones, but not enough. Mostly, they depended on rapid word of mouth and couriers.

"Group Cathy right behind us, moving left," passed up the line like a game of Gossip.

"Stay in position," a courier hissed back at Cathy's leader, galloping headfirst into their trench.

The field phone did tell Command that the right and left flanks were shaping up around the airfield, where a brace of sloppy-looking fighters—the same ones they had seen before?—made ineffectual guards for a group of plump personnel-and-supply-toting Ilyushins. These planes were in the way.

When the light was thickening with pre-dawn impenetrability, and Bo started seeing the planes and buildings as wobbling silhouettes, he heard it. Or them.

1.

If you had been alive in, say, 1492, and a B-29 flew overhead, how would you describe the sound? Or the Götterdammerung roar of a B-52?

Aircraft had been his life. But he hadn't heard the sound of a mass of them in so long, even *he* was awed.

They had let the prop jobs get a head start, he guessed. Because you heard them first, and then their rhythmic racket was drowned out by the whirlwind of jets, above and behind their formation.

On the ground, the Americans froze. They saw lights go on in the airport compound.

WHUMP! He had even forgotten to shield his eyes, and the blast blinded him, as the bomb blew the Russian radio hut to smithereens. His hand over his eyes, he heard the multiple detonations of the mines and felt the blasts of hot air, dirt, and gravel.

Between his fingers, he saw bright light. The starshells, the flares were a few minutes later than they should be. Or did the American air arm *plan* to destroy the radio shack before dropping them? The nightmare-white light of the flares reminded him of the time the Russkies hounded them from Ellaville. He laughed, and turned to see Juanita shrieking at the field phone operator.

"We go! Attack!"

She catapulted herself from their hiding place, running low. Squad Seven was right behind. Myron was screaming like a banshee, firing wildly. They threw themselves into a bomb crater, and peered to the next row of barbed wire and concrete barriers.

CRUMP! Returning fire—a mortar?—obligingly cleared the next fifty feet.

After their first bombing run, the American planes were circling overhead.

Christ, what if they hit *us* next time? Bo didn't know whether it was more vital to look ahead or up. He couldn't imagine any reason why they wouldn't, but they didn't.

Now the mortars and heavy guns had caught up with the first American wave, and they began to blow apart the airport defenses. Peering over the ragged crater edge, Squad Seven saw the field of fire trudge thunderously away from them, obliterating everything in its path.

There was a hundred yards clear in front of them. The General raised her gun and waved. "Forward!"

"Fah-wahhd!" Myron yelled on the right. "Fah-wahd!" somebody screamed on the left flank. He turned, running, and saw Bettina trotting stiffly at the head of the group.

When they dove into the next brand new trench, obligingly dug by the shell of an M20, he deliberately jumped on top of Juanita, gouging her with his knees, smashing her with his gun.

She didn't turn, or acknowledge his presence, his rebuke. He gritted his teeth through the next thunder of shells, and slipped off her.

The Russians were not as strong here as they had feared. Or they were caught by surprise. Or they were laying a trap.

The American Air Force—he could see it now—was making another bombing run. They came in so low—jets and propellor planes alike—that he could see the rising sun reflected on the bomb bay doors. Snuggled in the bombing group, a pair of antique Sabres did a little precision strafing in the Russian compound.

On the second circuit of the airport, when Russkies began to run out of the remaining buildings, the Sabres or some other planes dropped napalm, and the enemy became human torches. The torches jigged about for a few minutes, then fell over, still flaming.

The biggest plane—the one that circled like a giant vulture—did nothing. It stayed high, but from the sound he knew it was a B-52, the sound he'd felt in his sleep, from a score of patrols over the Atlantic.

Click. Puzzle pieces slipped together in his mind.

Juanita said they would use nuclear weapons to beat the Russkies. Drive them out.

And there she was, that beautiful, clean B-52, just sailing overhead, just low enough to get detailed ground recon. She was a bird made to deliver nuclear.

On the next assault, he could barely drag himself out of the crater. On impulse, he fell sideways, toward the squad Bettina led. He wriggled across the dirt and stones and debris, and found the old woman, reloading her M16 ecstatically, and wrapped an arm around her frail shoulders.

"It's going great!" She was suffused with an unnatural glow, and there was a mist of perspiration on her forehead and upper lip. Her pupils were pinheads.

"We're dead," he said flatly.

"Bullshit."

"No, look." He grabbed her chin and aimed it up at the giant jet. "B-52."

"Ours. I know. Terrific." She jerked her chin loose.

"Bettina, that bird is not bombing, not strafing."

"So?"

"So that's the nuclear stuff they were talking about. That's how she knows she'll die."

Bettina became enraged. "What the fuck are you talking about? We're winning! We don't need . . ."

"But we will. We will. Don't you get it?" He gave her a look of despair. "They don't think we can do it, Commander. They don't think we can win it at all."

Bettina's breast heaved with hyper-breathing. She inhaled and exhaled three times. "Sonny," she said, "you're paranoid. You've been around that woman too long."

She shrugged him off to talk to a courier, and Bo slithered back to his own group. Juanita turned around, and he could see flames from the burning building reflected in her eyes.

When the airport area was cleared and open, Phase II began.

Russian HQ was in the erstwhile shopping center on the other side of town. Rather than risk delay by a massed assault, they would use a commando group to cut directly through the heart of town, while the bulk of the troops executed pincer movements to the right and left.

Squad Seven was the commando group. At a brisk trot, they entered. It had been the black section of town, the slums, left to rot in old-fashioned, two-story clapboard disarray, while the glossier Valdosta of the New South grew up, around, and away from it.

Under the occupation, it was virtually deserted. A few shabby bars and seedy food shops were all they saw on either side of the railroad line. If any people lived here they were hiding. On her recon trip through town, the General had discovered you could slip through this section directly into the freight loading yards, and be hidden by the security fences there.

Squad Seven was silent, except for breathing. Myron was carrying the Commander piggyback style, and still keeping up. As they left the railroad depot, they could begin to hear the sounds of attack and combat, to their right and left. Mortars thumped. Machine guns played tattoos, and sirens the first they'd heard, began to wail. He guessed they had wiped out the airport sirens with their first attack. He looked up to see the planes again, but didn't.

Between the last of the rail yards and the HQ, they had to cross a large, open green, formerly John F. Kennedy Park, and then cut through a residential neighborhood. Juanita admitted she had no idea what they would encounter.

She held up a hand, meaning "wait." They listened, and then she signaled "forward." Squad Seven burst from their protected area onto the grass at top speed.

Across the park, they saw Russkies galloping out of their quarters buttoning their tunics, wives and screaming babies looking out the windows. Halfway across, a round of fire came at them from one of the houses, and Bettina yelled "Down!"

"That one." Bo spotted the house. Myron reached for the grenade gun, but Juanita was faster. She sprang into a kneeling position, fired, and the house exploded like a balloon.

There was no more attacking fire, just screams, and people ran out of their houses in terror.

Juanita was transfixed. Bo had to give the order to get the squad moving again. He swatted her with his gun to break her trance. She moved like a robot, but they ran across the rest of the green to the sanctuary of the trees and creek.

The creek obligingly led to a ravine deep enough to hide in.

Two of the men were hit. Bo determined that they weren't badly wounded, threw a first aid kit at the pair, and ran to catch up as the squad kept moving.

The gulch ran right beside and around the ex-mall. The Russkies were using it to dump garbage, and worse. Near the storm drains, the smell of shit filled the air.

"Christ, they're flushing their toilets into here."

"They don't have cesspools in Russia?"

"City sewers porbably don't work any more."

As they squelched along, fences and overgrown backyards—no dogs barking, he thought incongruously—turned into a shabby stucco wall.

The Valdosta Mall had been designed with a pseudo-Spanish motif. White stucco covered concrete block, and there were arches and phony wrought-iron railings and red-tiled roofs.

The mall's architect would have wept to see his creation now. Stucco did not weather well. Where it wasn't a dirty green-gray, it was gone altogether, exposing moldy concrete block. The effect was that of a decomposed corpse.

They were creeping up on the erstwhile freight entrance. It still said "Loading Dock 3" but the Russkies weren't taking supplies in here, that was for sure. Tiles were missing, windows gaped open, and moss grew in the fissures.

There was a rusted-out American halftrack where hundreds of eighteen-wheelers once had backed up and unloaded their cargos of hot dogs, instant hair setters, tape decks, and cork-soled wedgies.

The corrugated metal gates were down and locked.

"Blow 'em." Juanita signaled the heavy guns to the front. They knelt in a prayerful line.

"One, two, and . . ." she didn't say "fire," but did, and they were in unison.

The shells made such an inferno, they had to file one by one past the flames and red-hot metal, into the guts of Russian Headquarters.

2.

They had not caught the Russians by surprise here.

Most of the mall had long been empty, dotted with looted stores, gutted storerooms. Where there were new doors and windows with bars, the Russkies were keeping only supplies.

Abandoning caution, Juanita made straight for the heart of the complex, the Sears store with the radar dish. Squad Seven followed.

The Russian sentries had departed so fast there was a mug of the hot slop they called coffee at one side of the entrance, and a hunk of meat-topped bread on the other. The main door was open.

All of Squad Seven, Myron, Bo, and Bettina came to a halt. Juanita kept going, and ran right into the dark doorway. Bo tried to yell at her, but his throat wouldn't open. They fanned out around the entrance, from the Kitty Kelly shoe store to the Fotomat.

Juanita trudged out of obscurity and into view again. She looked disgusted.

"It's not HQ" she grunted. They all sat down and stared at the doorway.

"Just for communications, you mean?" Bettina's voice was raspy. She was breathing in gasps, and sweating heavily. "Let's take a look."

They went through a dark hallway to the brightly lit inner room. There were radio consoles, radar screens, still humming and pinging with life, and a strange kind of Telex system. It was not impressive. They had expected more, much more of the occupying power.

"Where are the big boys?"

"Beats my ass," Juanita said broodingly, and then she

brightened. "Well, the least we can do . . ." she gestured expansively, like a hostess trying to rescue a bad party, "the least we can do is trash it."

"Trash it!" Myron roared, and Squad Seven merrily wasted ammunition on the machines, at such short range it was a miracle nobody got killed by ricochet. After a few rounds, circuits began to short out, and blue arcs sizzled from one control panel to another.

"Generator's in here."

"Where?"

"Got it!" A blast and puff of smoke came from the next room, and everything went black.

"Myron?" Juanita's voice was deceptively gentle.

"Yes, Ma'am?"

"What does the radio advise?"

"Um," Myron answered. Bo could tell he'd been having so much fun, he'd forgotten all about communications with the main force. Recovering himself, Myron made a rapid retreat to the loading dock.

Out in the daylight, the radio operator and his aide were still huddled. The aide had a gun. The radio operator looked up at Juanita as she approached, and began to talk. Gibberish. But she was nodding, and gibbering back. The man pressed more buttons, and began to gabble into the mike. The radio answered in kind.

"Back to the airport!"

"What?" They looked at the General with dismay.

"I said, back to the airport. Find some truck or Russki cars."

In the garage they found an open Russian truck with a soft tire, hot-wired it, and were on their way.

The American planes—or something else—had wiped out the suburban neighborhood they'd come through. The passengers, jammed haunch to haunch in the back, were silent. The truck was driven by one Corporal Vaughn Belvin, with underworld expertise. The passengers were slammed from side to side, but they just looked at the General.

"We were attacked from the rear. At the airport," she yelled, but only half of them could hear, so the others were passed the word. "The mall was a phony. HQ's back there—or at least, they're holing up there. And they've got big stuff."

"Bomb them!" somebody yelled.

"The air squadron isn't here now. Refueling, re-arming, or something." Her face was a blank, and Bo saw the B-52, now circling almost out of sight.

Like most airports this one was located on flat, open, windswept ground. But the ground was rapidly becoming less flat, with shell craters and explosions.

The Americans were on the inside of the circle. Bad. They had nothing behind them but the ruins of fragile buildings. Poor shelter. No place to hide. And the Russkies were blowing holes in their existing lines.

Behind the Russian lines, on the other hand, were the woods, the highway, and the river. And they could still use the runway to escape, if any of their aircraft could fly.

Bo looked up again to see the American death bird, and it was there. The time to worry, he told himself, is when it's low enough to count the engines. Like the saying goes, when you see eight, it's time to rate. The shadow of the airport tower was growing longer across the pocked runways.

"Finish them," he heard Juanita say. She had assembled a line of gunners, and was pointing to the aircraft parked before them.

Shooting across the other fields of fire, Squad Seven did as they were told. For some reason, the propellor planes were more durable than jets: minutes after the more modern craft settled to the ground in flames, they still stood.

Incongruously, the American Air Force appeared again. But their information was out of date. They were strafing and bombing behind the fight, in parts of town nobody cared about.

But the result was that even more Russians flowed from the town afire behind them, into the airport.

As the squad crouched below the brush, the enemy swarmed on either side of them. Men, women, and children. Juanita extended both arms, palms down, signaling "Hold your fire." They maintained silence.

Wherever the rest of the U.S. Army was, it wasn't firing any longer. The Russians continued to stream to the control tower and waiting rooms. An unlit sign above the biggest building said "Eastern."

Juanita was gabbling to the radio operator again. "What now?" Bo asked querulously. "And what is that you're talking?"

"We attack at eleven hundred."

"Eleven hundred?" the Commander butted in. Her breath rattled, and she leaned heavily on her gun. Her skin was greasy and liverish.

"Right. And it's Latin."

"Hanh?"

"The code is our own version of Latin."

"Oh," Bo snapped. "Maybe you'll let us know where the rest of the American forces are."

"To our right and left. They took heavy losses."

"Fifty per cent," the radio man squealed. He had tears in his pale, rabbity eyes.

"Jeezus."

"How?" the Commander barked.

"The Russkies in the airport—mostly the tower—waited till we split up. Half an hour after Squad Seven moved out, they shelled from the rear."

They looked across the devastated runways and turf. Bo groped for the binoculars. With them you could see that some of the bumps on the ground were bodies. A lot of them. Smoke wisped across the scene, adding a further hellish touch. He tried desperately to remember the name of the Angel of Death. She had told him. Azriel, yes. Azriel was here.

And the death bird was circling, even before the vultures. He turned to ask if there was enough death for her. But she was impassive, locked in a trance.

The Commander was drinking from her canteen and swallowing some pills. The rest of the squad ate and drank, too. He heard people stirring and fidgeting all around him. His watch had stopped. Shock? Or a dead battery? He leaned to look at Myron's old-fashioned Omega, ticking away sturdily. Four minutes until they attacked.

The troops finished their meals, finished relieving themselves. (The women went modestly into the trees.) They were coiling up, flicking the bolts on their weapons, sliding the actions, fingering the triggers.

The radio man had the mike open, and you could hear the machine crackle and hum. Juanita raised an arm, and Bo and Myron and Bettina did likewise. They screamed "attack!" in perfect unison.

The Russians in the airport tower opened fire the instant they scrambled out of their hiding places.

3.

They tried five times.

Five times they swarmed up out of their pits and craters, right, left, and center.

But before they could gain enough ground to establish new lines, or even fire the heavy weapons, they would be driven back by precision fire from the Russian lines. Juanita was always the last to retreat, and did so slowly, but she was unwounded. The crater was filled with casualties, some living and some dead. Bo was weeping with rage, the Commander was animated and furious.

"Can't those cocksuckers on the right get a shell into the tower?"

"They're in range, I'd swear they are," Myron growled. But the right flank either didn't know they were in range, or were in no condition to take advantage of the fact.

Squad Seven had been forty men and women.

Subtracting the two they left in the gulch, in town, Bo counted less than twenty alive and functioning. Now Juanita was showing the first signs of agitation. She stood up and glared at the enemy.

"We're not going to make it, are we?" Bo asked.

She turned and glared at him. "Defeat is out of the question," she said almost primly, and leaned over the radio operator, who was dirtier, sweatier, and more scared than ever. "Call for help," she said softly. The squad stirred hopefully, everyone but Bo.

He looked up to the sky to see if death was approaching, but that wasn't where the noise came from.

The Americans had stopped firing. The Russians had stopped firing. What was that unearthly roar?

It came from behind the airport, behind the Russian lines, from the woods. It was SAM-7's and M16's and grenades and a banshee roar of hatred. It was the American civilians, the people from the *George Washington*. They had been let loose.

It took a number of amateurish shots, but the top of the airport tower disappeared in a puff of smoke and a shower of debris. With their vantage point gone, the Russian fire became disorganized. They tried to send troops around to the rear for defense, but it was too late. The mob was already there.

Civilians and troops alike, the Russians began to pour out of the buildings where they had taken refuge. Glass walls splintered, roofs collapsed, bricks flew. They milled around, and then began to run away from the new attack, toward the American lines. The ominous dark green uniforms ran just as fast as the dresses and suits. Several were waving white handkerchiefs at the uniformed forces they saw before them.

But the Americans from the rear swarmed over and through and around the wreckage. And caught them and pulled the Russians limb from limb. Literally.

Some of the enemy women and children managed to run away. The mob did not pursue them with the same fury as the men, which was not to say they did not slaughter the innocent.

The American military lines never fired. They ran toward the runways, and a few officers yelled "stop!" or "that's enough!" at the carnage, but, of course, it wasn't. The regular American soldiers just waited and watched, their presence blocking the last escape route. Bo thought of asking the General to order a stop. He turned and saw Juanita and Bettina, and knew neither would do so.

Bo saw a large black woman, wearing a cutoff sweatshirt that said "Atlanta Braves," kill a grizzled Russian soldier with a machete. He had been on his knees wiping blood from his eyes.

An elderly gentleman, with perfect if arthritic posture

carefully took aim and shot a Russian nurse in the back, as she ran away carrying an infant.

A teenage girl yelled, "Look! Look! He's escaping!" and pointed at the Russian officer as he ran. But nobody else heeded, so she ran after him, frantically digging inside her blouse. She pulled out the grenade, removed the pin and flung it after the Russian with a girlish gesture. But it was enough. The officer became a wet, red blur.

After some time—how long had the butchery gone on?— there were no more invaders left to kill. The mob let the American soldiers around up the few survivors and take them prisoner. Bo felt a bitterness at the back of his throat, and he vomited in the mud.

It was an immoral, vicious animal act to turn the mob loose to kill. But they had won. And he was alive, and he had expected to be dead. Wiping his mouth against a filthy sleeve, he ran to intercept Juanita as she entered the ruins of the tower.

"My condolences." She stared. "You didn't manage to kill yourself. And you didn't get to use your bomb."

Incredibly, she grinned. "My bomb? You mean the nuke I've got up in the B-52?" She pointed and he was horrified to see the jet was lower, lower in the sky. "I'll let you in on a little secret," she whispered archly. "There was no bomb. Is no bomb."

"No bomb?" he croaked. "Then what..."

"We never got one built. The scientists never got it together."

"Oh, shit!" he began to see what trouble they'd been in.

"Yeah. All we had was people, babe. All we ever had was people."

"Then what?" he cocked a finger at the big plane.

"Oh, it's coming in for a landing. A delegation from the High Command is arriving to set up a provisional government."

Bo giggled, and hugged her, much to her embarrassment. She groped inside her battered jacket, and pulled out a square, soft package.

The flagpole was in front of the passenger lounge, whose

bronzed glass walls now lay in shards on the ground. It was a good twenty-five feet tall, and the red flag, the hammer and sickle, taunted them from it.

The lines that raised and lowered the flag had been blown away. The crowd froze as they saw the General was going to climb it. She tucked the bundle back in her jacket, and began to shinny up, in full view of the whole field.

4.

He'd been in the men's room of the tower, urinating and dreaming of Russian girls, when the attack came.

Now the Russian non-com, Anatoly, was trapped. The bathroom door was sealed shut, blocked by debris from above. The ceiling threatened to give way at any moment.

The window gaped open, but he had seen enough. He had seen the Americans massacre his countrymen. Thank God his wife was at home in Voronezh.

Anatoly heard thumping and crashing below. They were working their way up. They would work their way in, and he would be butchered.

He looked out the window again.

There was a blond boy at the top of the flagpole. He was swinging with a knife. Slash! The beloved red flag collapsed like a rag. Slash! It fell from the top of the pole, and he followed it down with his gun barrel.

The man in uniform, an American officer, caught the flag in his outstretched arms and looked up.

The blond boy pulled something out of his jacket, and shook it open. Anatoly felt an instinctive chill. The boy was attaching the red, white, and blue flag, top end first, then bottom.

The crowd of Americans was quiet. Frighteningly so. As the American flag took the breeze, Anatoly looked down again. The American officer had dropped the red flag on the ground, and was grinding a heel into it, to cheers.

Anatoly fired.

He felt something wet hit his cheek.

He opened his eyes, it was easy, and saw Juanita above

him. Her face was contorted, but he recognized her. Amazing. She was crying. Her arms were around him, and she was crying and moaning and rocking back and forth. He wanted to tell her how surprised he was, but couldn't.

She leaned down and kissed him wetly, full on the lips. When she pulled away, he saw Bettina, crying, too.

It was a good scene. A being-loved scene. But it was getting further and further away.

The B-52 made a terrible, bumpy landing and taxied jerkily across the pitted macadam to the ruined airport buildings.

The staff aboard, and the provisional governament, were assaulted by heat and humidity as the doors opened. They didn't expect a big reception, but more than they got.

They crawled out of the plane, carrying their suitcases and portfolios and code boxes. Only a few of the American soldiers or civilians strolled over to look.

Most of the people—not as many as the provisional governor had expected—were in a circle around the flagpole, where the Stars and Stripes flew proudly. But the people were looking down. Down at two women—one old, one young—kneeling and weeping over the body of a man in uniform.

ABOUT THE AUTHOR

ALLYN THOMPSON lives in New York City. This is her first novel.

OUT OF THIS WORLD!

That's the only way to describe Bantam's great series of science fiction classics. These space-age thrillers are filled with terror, fancy and adventure and written by America's most renowned writers of science fiction. Welcome to outer space and have a good trip!

We Deliver!

And So Do These Bestsellers.

☐	20230	**THE LAST MAFIOSO: The Treacherous World of Jimmy Fratianno**	$3.95
☐	20296	**THE COMING CURRENCY COLLAPSE** by Jerome F. Smith	$3.95
☐	14998	**LISTEN AMERICA!** by Jerry Falwell	$3.50
☐	20700	**THE RIGHT STUFF** Tom Wolfe	$3.95
☐	20229	**LINDA GOODMAN'S SUN SIGNS**	$3.95
☐	01341	**NEWBORN BEAUTY: A complete beauty, health, and energy guide to the nine months of pregnancy, and the nine months after** by W. Gates & Gail Meckel	$9.95
☐	20483	**WEALTH AND POVERTY** by George Gilder	$3.95
☐	20198	**BOOK OF PREDICTIONS** by Wallechinsky & Irving Wallace	$3.95
☐	20082	**WHEN LOVERS ARE FRIENDS** by Merle Shain	$2.50
☐	13101	**THE BOOK OF LISTS #2** by I. Wallace, D. Wallechinsky, A. & S. Wallace	$3.50
☐	14638	**THE COMPLETE SCARSDALE MEDICAL DIET** by Herman Tarnover & S. Baker	$3.95
☐	05003	**THE GREATEST SUCCESS IN THE WORLD** by Og Mandino (A Large Format Book)	$6.95
☐	20558	**THE LORD GOD MADE THEM ALL** by James Herriot	$3.95
☐	20457	**ALL THINGS WISE AND WONDERFUL**	$3.95
☐	20456	**ALL THINGS BRIGHT & BEAUTIFUL**	$3.95
☐	20434	**ALL CREATURES GREAT AND SMALL** by James Herriot	$3.95
☐	14017	**THE SIMPLE SOLUTION TO RUBIK'S CUBE** by Nourse	$1.95
☐	22635	**THE THIRD WAVE** by Alvin Toffler	$4.50
☐	20621	**THE PILL BOOK** by Dr. Gilbert Simon & Dr. Harold Silverman	$3.95
☐	01352	**THE PEOPLE'S ALMANAC #3** by David Wallechinsky & Irving Wallace A Large Format Book	$10.95
☐	14500	**GUINNESS BOOK OF WORLD RECORDS—19th Ed.** by McWhirter	$3.50

Buy them at your local bookstore or use this handy coupon for ordering:

Bantam Books, Inc., Dept. NFB, 414 East Golf Road, Des Plaines, Ill. 60016

Please send me the books I have checked above. I am enclosing $_____
(please add $1.00 to cover postage and handling). Send check or money order
—no cash or C.O.D.'s please.

Mr/Mrs/Miss_____

Address_____

City_____State/Zip_____

NFB—3/82

Please allow four to six weeks for delivery. This offer expires 9/82.

FANTASY AND SCIENCE FICTION FAVORITES

Bantam brings you the recognized classics as well as the current favorites in fantasy and science fiction. Here you will find the beloved Conan books along with recent titles by the most respected authors in the genre.

☐	14428	LORD VALENTINE'S CASTLE Robert Silverberg	$2.95
☐	01166	URSHURAK Bros. Hildebrandt & Nichols	$8.95
☐	20156	BABEL-17 Samuel R. Delany	$2.50
☐	20063	GATES OF HEAVEN Paul Preuss	$2.25
☐	14844	NOVA Samuel R. Delany	$2.50
☐	20987	TRITON Samuel R. Delany	$2.95
☐	14861	DHALGREN Samuel R. Delany	$3.95
☐	20870	JEM Frederik Pohl	$2.95
☐	13837	CONAN & THE SPIDER GOD #5 de Camp & Pratt	$2.25
☐	13831	CONAN THE REBEL #6 Paul Anderson	$2.25
☐	14532	HIGH COUCH OF SILISTRA Janet Morris	$2.50
☐	20722	DRAGONDRUMS Anne McCaffrey	$2.50
☐	14127	DRAGONSINGER Anne McCaffrey	$2.50
☐	14204	DRAGONSONG Anne McCaffrey	$2.50
☐	20914	MAN PLUS Frederik Pohl	$2.75
☐	14846	THE GOLDEN SWORD Janet Morris	$2.50
☐	20592	TIME STORM Gordon R. Dickson	$2.95

Buy them at your local bookstore or use this handy coupon for ordering:

Bantam Books, Inc., Dept. SF2, 414 East Golf Road, Des Plaines, Ill. 60016

Please send me the books I have checked above. I am enclosing $_____ (please add $1.00 to cover postage and handling). Send check or money order —no cash or C.O.D.'s please.

Mr/Mrs/Miss_____

Address_____

City_____ State/Zip_____

SF2—1/82

Please allow four to six weeks for delivery. This offer expires 6/82.